CW00848434

# INGLES

# MANOR

S S Saywack

First published in 2022 by Blossom Spring Publishing
Inglestone Manor
Copyright © 2022 S S Saywack
ISBN 978-1-7396277-9-9
E: admin@blossomspringpublishing.com
W: www.blossomspringpublishing.com
Published in the United Kingdom. All rights reserved
under International Copyright Law.

*To all my family*
*for their support*
*over the years.*

25th November 1944, 12.26pm

New Cross Road, Deptford, London, SE14

168 people were killed and 123 injured when a V2

rocket destroyed Woolworths and the

Co-op next door.


**"At the going down of the sun and in the morning, we will remember them. R. I. P."**

*London, end of November 1944*

## Chapter 1

Less than a week after the bomb exploded in New Cross, Mrs Allen decided. Lizzy thought her mother had something important to say, going by her expression. As if to confirm her suspicions, when their maid, Susan, wearing the same glum expression, whispered, 'You be good, do you hear?' Lizzy knew it for sure.

At thirteen years old, Elizabeth was the eldest of the Allen children. Her mother had often told her she was the sensible one. Charlie was the middle child and wanted to be a Spitfire pilot when he grew up. At eight years old, Munch was the youngest. Many years ago, when Susan caught her eating some freshly made biscuits before they had time to cool, she called her *'Munch'*. The name stuck. Her actual name was May—or Katherine May, to be formal.

'Children, I need you to be brave. Just when I thought it was all over, now we have this to deal with after all the bombing and the blitzing,' Mrs Allen said later that evening.

'The rocket bombs?' Lizzy asked.

Mrs Allen nodded. 'And especially after what happened recently.'

'Do you mean at the Woolworths store?'

'What happened at Woolworths?' May asked.

'I told you,' Lizzy said. 'It's where the rocket bomb landed, and all those people died.'

'Oh, I thought you meant our Woolworths,' May mumbled and looked at the floor.

'No, Munch, the one in New Cross,' Mrs Allen said.

She had been nearby when the rocket bomb landed. The V2, they called it. It was one of Mr Hitler's vengeance weapons. Many died that day. She couldn't bear to think what would have happened if she'd stopped to buy the new saucepans they needed.

'I can't get it out of my mind. How were they to know a bomb would land there? It's funny, I've never cried since the start of this whole dreadful business—even after everything I've seen.'

Mrs Allen pulled May closer. After five years of war, she felt the fighting would never end. First, they had the blitz, then another blitz, and now a third. And now this tragedy in New Cross.

'But things are different from a few years ago. Then the Germans were bombing the East End mainly, and we were safe in our little cellar, so far from there. I know there was a lot of noise with the guns firing, and it made you cry sometimes, Munch.' She ran her fingers through the small girl's hair. 'And I know a few bombs fell near us. But it wasn't many, was it, children?'

They shook their heads.

'Susan was more scared,' Charlie said.

'Why was Susan more scared?' May asked.

'Susan lives in Poplar.' Lizzy said. 'That's in the East End. She said one night the German planes destroyed half of her street in one air raid.'

'Oh. Nobody tells me anything,' May murmured.

'That's the point, children,' Mrs Allen said. 'It took the Germans a whole air raid, with lots of aeroplanes dropping bombs to destroy Susan's street. But this bomb can do it in one go.'

Lizzy's gaze dropped. She had anticipated this—the population of her school had shrunk. The same thing happened four years ago. Like so many children, they'd been evacuated and stayed with a maiden aunt in the country to escape the bombing—the dragon. They despised her so much that Mrs Allen brought them home as soon as the bombing, dubbed the Blitz by everyone, ceased. But then it began again. And what was happening now, with the rocket bombs, was dreadful.

'The thought of one of those bombs landing on our house frightens me,' Mrs Allen told them. 'And I would never forgive myself if anything ever happened to you, if I could have prevented it.'

'You're going to send us away again, aren't you, Mum?' Lizzy said.

'Send us away?' Charlie and May cried in horror, remembering the last time they were sent away.

'But Mum, what about school? What about my friends?'

'Lizzy, I need you to be strong.' Mrs Allen spoke in a soft voice, but she was being firm. She took Lizzy's hands and squeezed them. 'I'm not taking this decision lightly. And it'll only be for a short while, just until the bombing stops. The school will still be there, and your friends will still be your friends. But you'll be safe. And I won't have to worry.'

Lizzy looked around, embarrassed—she knew how difficult this was for her mother and how much she needed her help. She heard the cry in her voice.

'I don't want to go,' a teary May said. 'We can always go down to the cellar when it comes.'

'Oh Munch,' Mrs Allen wiped away the tears from the girl's cheeks. 'I want to gather you all in my arms, hold you and never let you out of my sight. But if I did, my courage would evaporate. And where would I be? I'd worry about you the next day and the one after that. If anything happened, the thought of losing you is unbearable.'

'Are we going to auntie Clarissa?' May asked. She dreaded the answer, screwed up her lips, furrowed her brows and expected the worst.

Mrs Allen smiled.

'No, my darling, Munch, the dragon will not be eating any of you. I made other arrangements. Now, children, will you all be strong for me? And make daddy proud?'

They nodded.

Of course, there was no use in complaining, and Lizzy told them so afterwards in no uncertain terms.

'I'm not complaining. I just don't want to go. Christmas won't be the same somewhere else,' Charlie said.

No one considered they'd ever have to go, and if they did, it'd be before Christmas. With one exception in 1940, Christmas was always at 32 Saltdene Road.

'What about the butcher? He's always ill. Mrs Jones says he gets a touch of malaria. Maybe we could get a touch of malaria as well,' Munch said.

Lizzy wanted to laugh. The excuses that came that night after being told about their mother's plans, had reached the lofty heights of the absurd. There was an unmistakable seriousness on the small girl's face, and Lizzy composed herself so as not to upset May.

'It's winter. Mosquitoes don't like the cold, and anyway, there aren't any in England.'

'Oh, I know,' May said, jumping on the bed.

'Hush, that's enough from both of you. We have to go, and that's final. So, no more talk about getting ill, running away, or whatever else,' Lizzy said.

They gave silent nods.

'Do you know where we're going?' Charlie asked.

'Somewhere north. Inglestone, or something or the other. Mum said it's not far from Leeds. Other kids are going, so we won't be alone. Susan said, it's a long train journey, and we should get there by early evening.'

'And there'll be no bombs?' May asked.

'Of course not. Why do you think we're going in the first place?' Charlie rolled his eyes.

'I know that.' May huffed and glared at him. She pursed her lips and folded her arms.

'Will you two shush? Come on, get into bed before mum comes. And listen. She's got enough on her plate. And when we go to the train station tomorrow, you're both going to be nice. Do you hear me? And don't you dare cry, Munch—that goes for you as well, Charlie— it'll only upset her. We might be sad about leaving, but what do you think Mum feels like?' Lizzy had heard enough.

May and Charlie mumbled a promise and climbed into bed, but they were still grumpy.

# Chapter 2

The next day, they went to the railway station. Lizzy had expected to see a great swathe of children waiting to be taken away, just as it was that first time they were evacuated. However, this was 1944. Many children who left at the start of the war were still with their evacuation parents, nevertheless, the platforms were full.

Despite her disappointment at leaving, Lizzy was thrilled. The air buzzed with excitement, and she was electric with anticipation. Her eyes flicked around as new sights caught her attention. Porters hurried everywhere. Great clouds of white steam hissed from the black train engines waiting beside the platforms. Their shrill whistles stung the air. Occasionally, the Tannoy crackled into life, and a nasal woman's voice echoed around the great open space.

Lizzy watched her brother and sister as they queued, to see they didn't get lost. She held Charlie's hand, and he held May's. She, in turn, held Susan's hand. Her thoughts went to the time May got lost in the crowded underground station during an air raid. It had been her job to look after May, but she'd fallen asleep. She woke in a panic and ran along the platform to find her sister, who had wandered off. She was crying when she heard the familiar voice of Susan and saw her lifting May into the air, swinging her around and saying, 'Got you, you little vixen,' and May's uncontrollable giggles.

'Now listen,' Susan said. The seriousness in the maid's manner brought home that they were leaving. 'Be brave for your mum's sake. You've got everything you need.' She tapped one of the suitcases the children carried. 'Fresh knickers. Stockings and socks, you've got two pairs of those, and the ones you're wearing. Some handkerchiefs—don't make them too snotty before you change them—vests, slips, a blouse and a warm cardie. You've also got pyjamas and your coats.' She pulled May's tighter around her. 'That'll keep you warm, Munch—It's bloomin' cold up north.'

'You've got your gloves, ain't you? You got a comb, a towel, toothbrush and a face cloth—you make sure you use them, otherwise I'll come and give your bottoms a spank. Oh, and keep those sandwiches in your coat pockets, so's you can get to them quick like. There's a couple of apples there as well and some raisins. And here, this is for you, Munch. Some of me biscuits. Made fresh mind. You share them with Lizzy and Charlie, you hear?'

Susan gave May a grave, theatrical stare, and May bit her lips to stop crying.

'An' don't you let me hear anything bad about you.' She waggled a finger at them all, but especially at Charlie. 'You lot ain't seen Susan in a temper before, but by heck, she can be a right little demon when she wants to.' She turned her face, blew her nose into a handkerchief, and wiped her eyes on her sleeve. 'Bloomin' sooty trains, smoke gets everywhere, don't it? And don't take this off.' She tugged a tag threaded through one of the button eyelets on May's coat. Each child had a similar tag. 'It says who you are and where you're from in case you gets lost. But you ain't gonna get lost because Lizzy's gonna look after you, ain't you, girl?'

Lizzy nodded weakly.

'And write your mum. And you can add a note to me in it as well if you like. And Lizzy, you've got the ration cards, don't lose them. Bloomin' pain in the bum if you do. Me old man lost his and—well, that's for another day, init?'

Susan hugged the children, gathering them into her

arms and squeezing them tightly, 'You look after them, Lizzy. And be good, Munch. And you be nice, Mr La-de-da.' She gave Charlie a wink.

A guard blew a sharp blast on his whistle. He said something about Inglestone and pointed to a train, with people moving towards it.

Mrs Allen took Lizzy aside.

'Now Lizzy, look after Charlie and Munch. They'll be pains, but we know that, don't we? Remember, you're the eldest. It's up to you to be me. It's you they'll be looking to. Put this in your purse.' She placed two folded five-pound notes inside. 'For emergencies. Every now and then, give the others a treat. All the arrangements have been made for when you reach Inglestone. The woman you're staying with is doing us a favour, so remember that. She contacted Aunt Marie where she works in billeting and asked for you three specifically.'

'Do we know her, mum?' Lizzy asked.

'That's the curious thing, Lizzy, we don't. So I don't know how she knows us. I suspect Aunt Marie told her. But this way, I can keep you all together and safe.'

The tannoy blared an announcement. Their train was departing in five minutes.

She gave Lizzy a kiss and a hug and did the same with the others before they went to the carriage. Lizzy found seats and stowed their suitcases. Her mother smiled from the platform and pretended to look happy.

Lizzy knew she wasn't. Nevertheless, she returned a confident smile as a lump rose in her throat, and a knot tightened her stomach. She wanted to grab May and Charlie and drag them off the train. They wouldn't fight her, and they could all go home for tea and toast. It would be so easy. But she was the eldest, and she had to do what was asked of her. She bit her lip and took a deep breath.

The whistle sounded. Great puffs of white steam erupted as the wheels screeched against the rails, grey-black smoke spurted from the funnel, and the train jerked once, then lurched off.

The children waved, and Mrs Allen and Susan waved back. Lizzy watched as the figures on the platform got smaller until they disappeared when the train rounded the first bend. She relaxed into her seat. May and Charlie sat silently with unsmiling faces. Lizzy wanted to say something, but no words came. She was afraid of the responsibility given to her and felt nervous. She listened to the noise of the engine and the wheels grinding on the steel rails, sounding out a plaintive beat, knowing that with each clack, the train was carrying them away from their home in London.

# Chapter 3

It was a long and torturous journey, made worse by the train stopping on numerous occasions for no apparent reason. Time was spent on sidings, and longer stops were made at various stations where nobody could get off. Through the window, they saw the changing landscape as the train took them further away. In some towns, the train slowed to a snail's pace, while destruction caused by the air raids lay all around them. Black burnt-out buildings reduced to hollow shells were stark against the sky, while piles of bricks had been gathered into great heaps on either side of the tracks. The children glued their faces to this new sight, fascinated by the destruction. For the first time, they saw first-hand that it wasn't just their city that had suffered the cataclysm. It was everywhere.

The journey was tiring, and soon May and Charlie dozed. When they woke up, Lizzy said they could eat their sandwiches. Later, she let them have the apples and then the raisins, and when they were gone, and they were peckish, May gave them Susan's biscuits. There was nothing left to eat when it was gone, and it was still early afternoon.

By evening, in the blacked-out carriages, Charlie and May succumbed to the sleepy, rocking rhythm of the train. Lizzy kept watch over them before dozing herself.

Outside, the landscape changed from open fields to dark heathland and sparse moors; a landscape with which she wasn't familiar. It looked inhospitable, cold and alien, a hard edge against the dark sky of the horizon.

'Where are we?' Charlie yawned and stretched his arms high.

'I don't know. I saw a sign that said Riddlington a while back, but I don't know where that is.' Lizzy tried not to sound downbeat, but it was a struggle.

'I'm hungry.'

'Me too. I think we're nearly there. Someone said that it's only an hour away, but that was forty minutes ago. Not long now.'

Before long, the train eased into a cold granite station. Chiselled into the granite was the name, *'Inglestone, 1860'*. In the dark December evening, it looked bleak and unwelcoming. It had seen better days, and the paint peeled from the frames of grimy, soot-covered windows.

What was left of the children—only a handful, disembarked. Most of them had already got off at earlier stops. When it had burped them onto the freezing platform, the train continued its slow journey into the night.

The Allens followed the others to a large hall. The air was cold, much worse than in London, and they felt the chill stealing their warmth.

Inside the brightly lit hall, someone was checking the children's nametags. When they found Lizzy, the three of them were ushered away to stand in a corner on their own.

The rest of the children were parcelled out to the various adults in the waiting room. There was an exchange of conversation, a check of tags, and then they left with their new people. Each time it happened, and it wasn't for them, Charlie and May looked at Lizzy. She stood firm and stony-faced, exuding just enough confidence to put them at ease. Soon, though, the hall emptied, and they were the only ones left, still standing alone in the corner.

It was Lizzy's turn to be worried.

She was nervous when the desk was cleared, and the officials had drifted away. The thought that they'd been forgotten loomed in her tired mind. She wondered if something had gone wrong with her mother's plan.

'I didn't expect to see you here tonight, Ted.' A plump woman in a green cable knit sweater spoke to a policeman who entered the hall.

He was the oldest policeman Lizzy had ever seen. His hair was white, and his face wrinkled with a ruddy complexion. His deep blue eyes were piercing. He rubbed his hands vigorously along his arms and stamped his feet a few times.

'Aye, well, three more's run away from Holcombe House—a boy and two others this time,' he moaned, taking off his helmet and wiping his forehead.

'Do you blame them, Ted?' The woman's lips pursed into a complaint. 'The things they do to them there is it any wonder?'

'It's not up to me to tell them how to do their job.'

'More's the pity.'

'They need to get that gate fixed. Anyways, it makes for a long night.'

He looked around the room and saw the Allens. Smiling as he approached them, he said, 'What have we here, then?'

He squatted down with difficulty and looked at their

nametags, shouting their names. The plump woman scrolled through a list. When she found them, she shouted back.

'Billy Gains, Ted. For old Miss Inglestone.'

'Billy Gains?' the policeman responded with scepticism. 'For Miss Inglestone?'

'Aye, that's what it says here.'

'All three?'

'Aye, for Miss Inglestone.' She tapped the list.

'Well, that's a first.'

'Appears as if she's asked for them specially. It says that here.'

'Ask for them specially? Since when do people do that? What does she want with them?'

'Who knows about dotty Dot? She's doolally, that one.'

May cast a nervous glance at Charlie and Lizzy.

'Now, now Milly. Dorothy's none of that.'

The plump lady huffed, muttering something no one else could hear.

'Well, seems you're going with Billy Gains when he comes, to her that lives in the lodge,' he said to Lizzy. 'It's a big house, plenty of legroom, more than enough for you short ones. Aye, Billy will be along soon. Here, Milly,' he shouted to the plump lady, 'you got any biscuits left? I dare say these pups are hungry and could do with a feed. They need something to keep their strength up.'

'Eh, ducks, of course, come here and have some of these.' She beamed a motherly smile and held out a saucer with half a dozen biscuits. The Allens were happy to get something to eat, even if it was only a few biscuits. They gulped them quickly, and May reached out to take another one.

'Eh, now. Leave me the plate, luv. You can't eat that, you know.'

May's mouth fell open, and Lizzy pulled her nearer, saying, 'Thank you very much, Miss.'

'Well, there's nowt like a good bit of manners, is there Ted. My pleasure, young lady.' She gave Lizzy a respectful nod.

A few more minutes passed before the door to the hall opened again. A large, heavy-set man came in with the rush of cold air. He was dressed in a dark, grimy coat, tied at the waist with a length of rope, and wore grey-black trousers and black boots caked in mud. A dark flat cap was pulled down his unshaven face. From under its shadow, his deep-set eyes, topped by bushy eyebrows, scanned the room. He was perhaps fifty years old. It was easy to imagine that he must have been a muscular, well-built man in his youth, and he still carried himself with a hint of that poise. However, he puffed as he walked, breathing heavily as if he'd rushed there. In the crook of his arm, he held a broken shotgun. He gave them a curious stare when he spotted the children but said nothing.

'Ay-up, Billy,' said the policeman, 'Milly were going to send out a search party for you.'

The man nodded and turned to the plump woman.

'These 'em?'

'They are,' Milly said. 'Elizabeth, Charles and May Allen.'

May looked at Charlie, and they shuffled closer to their sister. Staring at the man, their mouths had gone dry.

Lizzy placed a hand on their shoulders to steady herself as the man stood in front of her. His breath smelled beery. There was something of a sneer on his lips. Then he sniffed, shook his head and turned away.

'Them's famished,' said the plump woman.

'There's grub at Lodge.'

'Well, you better sign here and take them away then.'

He signed with a bandaged hand and walked to the door.

'Well, you coming? We'll have to leg it. This ain't the city, no buses 'ere. Name's Gains. Mr Gains.'

'Yes, Mr Gains,' Lizzy said, and the others mumbled the same as they followed him.

Seeing the smaller ones struggling with their cases, Milly shouted, 'You could give them a hand, Billy Gains.'

'I dare say they'll manage,' he said without looking back.

'Ever the gentleman, aren't you, Billy?'

'Still looking for treasure, Billy?' said the policeman.

Bill Gains shot him a look of contempt and curled his lips in an ugly way. The policeman snorted a laugh and looked at the plump woman, who turned away to avoid being seen laughing.

# Chapter 4

It was an unpleasant walk to the lodge along a rough path that climbed into the gloomy darkness. Lizzy carried hers and May's suitcases, while the other two took turns with Charlie's. Though the air was cold, they soon warmed up, especially as Mr Gains set a decent pace. At times they had to run to keep up. But they did it without complaint, not sure how they should address the hulking gentleman yards in front of them.

Rain had fallen during the day, soaking the ground into mud. The children slipped and slid in their city shoes. The path was rutted, and it was a challenge to avoid stepping into one of the deep furrows in the darkness. They stumbled into one more than once and felt the icy ankle-deep water pinching their toes. Every time Lizzy looked up, she saw Mr Gains, with his head bent and walking with purpose. Behind her, May and Charlie trudged along, puffing hard as they neared a house that had loomed into view.

'Just top of lane,' Mr Gains said without looking back or breaking stride.

Lizzy wanted to ask him to slow down, but she was

nervous of the man, and her courage failed. She smiled encouragement at Charlie and May, and trusting in her, they smiled back as they struggled along.

Apart from the once Mr Gains spoke, it was deathly silent. Lizzy heard little as they marched, their footsteps on the path, the splashes when they stepped in a puddle and her breathing hard. That, and the frantic beat of her heart. When nature did speak to them, it was wild. The wind's keening whistle across the moors rose to a pitch and dropped off before the next gust, blowing her hair into a tangle. When she was hot, the wind crept under her collar and pinched her sweat-wet neck, chilling her to the bone in seconds.

The building rose like a beast from the darkness, a black shape against a dim sky. Behind that loomed another structure that was darker still. It gave the impression of being bigger than the house.

Before long, they were standing by a door under a small porch. They were panting from their exertions and relieved to put down the burden of their suitcases.

Mr Gains threw open the latch and walked into a kitchen. A blast of warm air and a drab yellow light surrounded the Allens. Lizzy ushered them inside, remembering the blackout rules, and they stood in silence behind the door. Before she had a chance to close it, Mr Gains pushed past her. Muttering something about them being born in barns, he gave the door a shove, and it banged hard against the frame.

At a cooker in the corner, a small woman turned around. She sniffed and turned back to her pots after seeing who had come in.

Lizzy looked around as a deep depression seeped into her heart. She glanced at May and Charlie, like her, they were looking around at their new home with a worried expression. There was no joy in this place. It was dark, dismal, and dirty, unlike their kitchen at 32 Saltdene Road. It smelt funny, with a rank odour, like vegetables long past when they should have been thrown away.

A lone bulb hung from the ceiling, and it cast an insipid yellow light that created murky shadows. There was a large table and four chairs under the light on a rough stone floor. The table was covered with a glossy worn oilcloth draped down the sides. A deep sink in a long cluttered worktop was under the window, and a gas-fired water heater hung above the sink.

'Those 'em? The ones she asked for?' the woman said.

'Aye,' Mr Gains walked to a corner and hung his shotgun on a hook.

'They can have supper before bed.'

She ladled steaming soup into three bowls and brought them to the table.

The children all said thank you, though Lizzy had to nudge May to get her to speak.

'You gonna eat standing up?' the woman said before turning back to the stove. The sharpness of her voice made Lizzy jump.

Lizzy ushered everyone to sit without speaking. They still had their coats on. The woman was about to say something, but she snorted instead and put three spoons on the table with a clatter.

The soup looked pleasant enough, unlike their hosts. Lizzy thought it was odd that they hadn't spoken to them, and she felt too unsure of herself to start a conversation. The soup was cloudy and milky, and some large potatoes protruded like islands from the steaming liquid, surrounded by what she took to be barley. It smelled delicious, and they hadn't eaten properly since their sandwiches earlier. Lizzy handed out the spoons and said another weak thank you to the woman. The reply was a grunt that Lizzy took to as acknowledgement.

'For tomorrow,' Mr Gains said.

He lifted something from under his coat on the counter and dropped it with a thump on the surface. When he walked away, May gasped in astonishment. Her mouth dropped, her eyes opened wide in horror, and the spoon fell with a splash into the soup.

On the counter, bedraggled and limp, with its head hanging down, was a rabbit. It had congealed blood around its mouth, and the grey fur was a wiry tangle. May froze—the dead eyes were open and seemed to be looking at her.

The woman saw the animal and carried on cooking.

Lizzy gave May a kick under the table, and the young girl looked at her in fright. She ate like a whipped puppy with her eyes lowered to the bowl, afraid to look up. Lizzy gave Charlie a reassuring look, and he also began eating, his eyes low as well. Each took care to avoid looking at the rabbit on the counter.

'Want some supper?' the woman asked the man.

'Later.'

He scrubbed his face at the sink with his hands and dried himself on a towel on a nearby hook.

'What you going to do with the toffs?' he asked.

'Get 'em to bed. They can see the old woman in the morning. You going out again?'

'Maybe. I thought I saw something by the old servant's quarters. I wanted to look at it again.'

'Best do that in the light.'

He thought for a second and nodded.

'Aye, dare say you're right.'

Lizzy, Charlie and May were hungrier than they realised, and the soup was soon gone. Lizzy figured that asking for seconds wasn't a good idea when she was down to her last piece of potato. She fished it out with her spoon and put it in May's bowl.

# Chapter 5

'You can see the mistress in the morning,' the woman growled as she led them along a dark corridor through the cold house. She held a candle, but the blinking flame shielded by her palm only gave meagre light. It was barely enough to light the way.

'The mistress?' Lizzy asked.

'Mistress sleeps there,' she gestured to a door at the end of the corridor. 'Your bedroom's this way.' She flicked her head to the staircase.

Lizzy looked at the door. Was she in there, the one Milly spoke about? The doolally one. Was she the one her mother made arrangements with? She was concerned. If a mistake had been made, she didn't know how to correct it. Seeing Charlie and May's faces worried her too. They looked horrified.

As they climbed the staircase to the landing above, Lizzy made out paintings on the walls in the flickering light, grey-brown things suggesting landscapes and flowers, and heavy old furniture against the walls. Underfoot, the carpet felt thin and threadbare. The floorboards creaked into a choir of squeaks from so many people walking across them at once. And like the kitchen, the hallway smelled musty and damp, it needed airing.

'This'll be yours. Breakfast at seven—I'll give you a call. There's candles and matches there. Bathroom and the whatnot are at the end of the corridor.'

She lit another candle with the flame from the dwindling one and turned away.

Lizzy saw an unshaded lightbulb hanging from the ceiling. She flicked the light switch by the door, but nothing happened.

The room was sparse. There were two beds, a single and a double, pushed against the walls. They were neat and made up, with the blanket at the top folded back, revealing white sheets. The floor had a tattered carpet, and the walls were bare except for an old landscape that was difficult to see in the gloomy light of the candle. Behind a blackout curtain, there was a large window. The chilly fingers of the wind clawed through cracks in the frame, and the curtains fluttered with every gust. There was an old wardrobe against one wall with a matching vanity, chair, and large mirror. On the far wall was the black ironwork shadow of a fireplace.

May couldn't take anymore and sobbed without daring

to make a noise. She dropped her suitcase in the centre of the room, wiping her nose with her sleeve.

Lizzy understood. It had been a long and horrible day. The house was gloomy and strange, and the people were stranger still. She knew May wanted to be at home, hearing her mother and Susan's voices in her familiar room surrounded by her toys. She longed to sleep in her own little bed. Lizzy was annoyed that she didn't know how to calm her sister. There was nothing she could do when she felt the same wretchedness.

'Cut that out.' She picked up the suitcase and pushed it away from the weeping girl.

'I want to go home. Please can we go home, Lizzy?'

'So, do I,' Charlie said.

They looked at her with pleading eyes, their arms hung limply by their sides, and tears wet their cheeks.

'I don't like it here.' May blubbered. 'Lizzy. It's not nice. I want mum. Can we go home, now?'

Lizzy looked at them crying and felt guilty for taking her frustration out on them. She sat May on the bed and pulled Charlie over. She put her arm around May's shoulders and gave her a warm hug while squeezing Charlie's hand the way her mother had squeezed hers.

'Shush. It's okay, Munch. I know it looks terrible. But it's just first impressions. Remember what Daddy said about first impressions? In the morning, it'll look a lot better. I promise, you'll see. It's just dark, we can't see anything, and it's all strange, that's all. Come on, dry those tears, for Mummy's sake. It'll be okay, Munch.'

Lizzy gave her a beaming smile, even though she felt the same depression and overwhelming desire to be anywhere else.

'Come on, you two, be brave. We're all tired. It's been a long day, hasn't it? And we're gonna sleep on it, aren't we?'

They nodded, but it was a mechanical gesture.

'Good. We're going to stick together and be good for Mummy, aren't we?'

They nodded again, but their eyes held a burning hope that they could leave.

'The Allens—one for all and all for one. The three Mouseketeers—Mouseketeer Charlie and Mouseketeer May.'

Lizzy waved an imaginary sword in the air. Susan would have handled this better. The maid was good in these situations, and she was just a child. May and

Charlie managed to give a small smile among their drying tears.

'And Mouseketeer Lizzy.' May's voice was hoarse as she hugged her sister, pressing her wet face against Lizzy's shoulder.

'And tomorrow we'll have a gander, a good look-see,' Lizzy said, imitating Susan's East End accent.

May and Charlie smiled.

'Come on, we can unpack tomorrow when there's more light. You two sleep here.' Lizzy tapped the double bed. 'And I'll be over there. Find your night things. Here Munch, let me help you.' She rummaged through May's suitcase. 'Come on, chop-chop. Coats off, shoes under the bed. Quick now. It's too cold to hang about. Dry your feet. Give your toes a rub.' They got up and took their coats off. 'Leave them on the chair, make a pile. We'll sort everything out tomorrow.'

They'd slipped out of their shoes and pulled off their jumpers when Lizzy said, 'What's this?' Her hand was inside May's suitcase.

She pulled out May's nightie wrapped around a fluffy if scruffy, black teddy bear.

'Look, Munch.'

May had forgotten Mr Fu-Fu in the excitement of leaving—but Susan hadn't. May's face brightened.

'Good old, Susan,' Lizzy said. 'Oh, my Munch, and what's this?'

Lizzy found a greaseproof paper bag. She burst out laughing, recognising the odour coming from inside. It was the distinctive smell of cinnamon. On the bag, Susan had written:

*For Munch – Merry (early) Christmas. Eat me now!*

Inside were three biscuits dotted with raisins. Lizzy handed the parcel to May, who shared them out. In the light of a flickering candle, they ate Susan's cinnamon-flavoured present in the cold, sparse bedroom.

The biscuits did the trick. Calm and more cheerful, Charlie and May slipped under the chilly sheets, tucked their legs up, and huddled closer against the cold.

'Good night, Munch,' Lizzy said.

May replied with a good night to her sister.

'Good night, Charlie.'

Charlie reciprocated.

Charlie then said goodnight to May.

In their tiredness, they quickly fell asleep.

## Chapter 6

It was still dark when Lizzy woke up. She spent a few minutes in the warm bed and contemplated the awful evening. However, now that her mind was clear and she was rested, she wanted to make the best of the situation. After all, they had no choice.

She washed and woke the others. May and Charlie yawned and tried to curl back into bed. The room was as cold as the night before, and with a bit of gentle shoving, they got up reluctantly. They tip-toed to the bathroom to wash. At least there was hot water to make it comfortable. When they came back to the bedroom, Lizzy had emptied their suitcases into two untidy piles. The wardrobe and vanity drawers were open. She was putting their clothes inside.

Nobody spoke much, and they were joyless and uncomfortable in the unfamiliar surroundings. However, it was time to get on with it. Under Lizzy's instructions, they helped to put things where she had allotted space for them. Clothes went into the wardrobe, shoes and boots into the corner behind the door, and coats hung on the hooks. They arranged their combs and hairbrushes on the vanity, making it look more like a lived-in room. They made their bed with Lizzy's help, smoothing out creases in the blanket, turning the top back, and fluffing the pillows—army-style, as Lizzy called it. Then they placed their folded night clothes under the pillows.

When they finished, they lined up at attention. May, unable to suppress her giggles, put her hand across her mouth as Lizzy walked along, adjusting their wayward clothing as if she was inspecting the troops. When she was satisfied, she pulled the blackout curtain back.

The window was streaked with condensation running into a puddle on the inside sill. She rubbed the mist away, clearing a patch like a ship's porthole with her fingers. The light was arriving, and the sky that had been grey and cloudy the evening before was bright. It would be a clear day, and the sun slanted over the land, tingeing it with a warm orange wash. Harsh swathes of deep shadows fell across the bushes, and the gorse sparkled with frost in the growing light. The wind had dropped away, and in the still calm, it seemed nothing stirred, except in the far distance, where lonely birds fluttered across a pale sky.

In the morning light, things were better.

'It looks lovely outside, but oh my, it's cold,' Lizzy

rubbed her hands to warm them.

'What are we doing today?' Charlie asked.

'We can explore a bit, and then we'll explore a bit more.'

Lizzy wanted to say something about making the best of things but thought it would remind them how they felt the night before. None of them needed reminding of their first impression. 32 Saltdene Road was far away, and it might be a while before they saw Susan's cheery face again. She already missed her stories about her *old man* and longed to hear the key turning in the front door to see their mother in the hallway. They had to find out where they were before getting used to being there.

'We're all on our own, and there's no houses,' May was peering out of the window.

'I saw one,' Charlie said, 'or I thought I did when we came.'

'Yes, me too. But I couldn't see much in the dark. It looked big, though. And the village is only a walk away. There's plenty to see there, Munch.' Lizzy tried to quell May's panic. She wasn't used to the solitude of the country.

'And look what I found, May. I wondered why my

case was so heavy.'

Lizzy lifted up two substantial books—the last two volumes of War and Peace, much to everyone's delight.

It was their mother's tradition to read to them before bedtime. She'd done it since their father left, first to North Africa in 1942 and then to Europe during the D-Day landings. Barring one week when he'd come home on leave, she'd never missed an evening. The grand story of War and Peace was halfway through, and their favourite character, Pierre, had arrived at a battle called Borodino.

'Now we can see how it ends. But I don't read as well as Mum. I can't pronounce the names like she does in that Russian way—*Anna Mik-hay-lov-na.*' She giggled.

'No, it's *Mick-hey-love-na,*' Charlie said. He laughed as he tried his Russian accent.

May attempted the word, and her tongue got tangled up, and it came out as a stutter, making them laugh as she tried again, and then a third time, with similar results.

'We can call her Anna,' May said.

'No, we can't. It's got to be the Russian way. Like this.' In a passable Russian accent and a deeper voice, Charlie said, 'Presenting the Princess Katherina May

Allenova and the Countess Elizabeth Sarah Allenova,' to his sister's delight.

'And we'll read a chapter each night,' Lizzy said.

'Yes, and it'll be great fun in the candlelight, won't it, Lizzy?' Charlie agreed.

Lizzy looked at the two volumes. Mother was telling her their stay might be a long one. But she kept the thought to herself.

A rap on the door startled them. The door opened, and the woman from the night before came in. She seemed surprised that they were awake, the curtains drawn and beds made. She hesitated, regained her composure, scowled and said, 'Breakfast's downstairs.' She left the door open behind her.

With the reminder of where they were, their hearts sank.

## Chapter 7

The kitchen was as depressing as the night before. In the daylight, it was clear why. It was still a dark room, but Lizzy noticed the peeling wallpaper, dirty walls, and the dark, greasy patch on the ceiling above the stove. The flagstone floor was grimy in places. The window was streaked with condensation gathering in a puddle on the inside sill; the paint was cracked and peeling at the edges.

Three plates were ready on the table, each with two slices of toast and a saucer of butter. They had eggs in three eggcups and beside each dish was a glass of milk.

The Allens went to the same chairs they occupied the night before. May and Charlie glanced at the counter. The rabbit was gone, but May looked around as if she expected to see it in a corner, watching her. They gave each other a sheepish look of comfort and solace. They ate quietly, but the treacherous toast crunched loud in the otherwise silent room.

The woman moved about the kitchen, doing chores as she went. She was in her fifties, stout and not tall. She wore a floral dress and a floral apron that clashed. Her dark chestnut hair was pulled back and tied in a tight bun, exposing the fullness of her face that hinted at how pretty she used to be. But the beauty had faded from her cheeks. She had a surly, unsmiling look and walked with a stoop.

'Bacon and eggs twice a week.' She spoke with her back to them, standing at the sink washing up. She was efficient, and the dishes stacked up. 'You'll have to make do with toast with jam or butter for rest. Cheese's plenty. Milk as well. I'll need your ration books. Sweet's once a month. Make sure you take care 'caus there's nowt till then. We do okay for meat. There's plenty of game on the moors.' Her voice was curt, staccato, and to the point.

'I'm Elizabeth,' said Lizzy, 'this is…'

'I know who you are. She's talked about you three often enough.'

'Talked about us? Who did?' asked Lizzy.

'There's chores to do,' the woman said, not bothering to answer. 'I'll tell you what they are later—we make do and mend in this house. Nowt's for free. School's closed 'til January as Mrs McKenzie's poorly and they can't find anyone to stand in for her. You'll have to amuse yourselves in-between times. When you finished, old Miss Inglestone wants to see you.'

'Old Miss Inglestone?' Lizzy asked.

'Aye. She wot owns lodge.'

'Oh. We didn't know.'

'Well, you do now.'

Lizzy glanced at Charlie and May. They looked cold and frightened. This woman didn't talk—she barked every word at them.

'Is it possible to light a fire in our room, please?' Lizzy asked. 'It was very cold this morning.'

'You can light a fire, can't you? You can have some coal every second day but nowt of a Saturday.'

Lizzy had never laid a fire, but she'd seen Susan do it and was familiar with the theory. The others looked at her for reassurance. She returned a confident smile.

'Sheds in't yard—only take a bit. The newspaper's in't cupboard.' The woman nodded to a cupboard by the wall. 'Kindling's outside, matches on't shelf. Candles in't drawer over there.'

When they'd finished eating, the woman gathered the plates and glasses and took them to the sink. As she rinsed them, she muttered loud enough for Lizzy to hear that they would do their own tomorrow.

An uncomfortable silence followed.

May glance around the kitchen. Her curiosity made

her restless, and she fidgeted. She swung her legs and then, with a smile, asked, 'Has Mr Gains found any treasure?'

The woman turned around sharply and glowered at the small girl.

'What d'you know about that?'

May jumped, and her gaze dropped to the table. She looked as though she was going to cry.

'The policeman said something,' Lizzy was stuttering.

There was an odd look on the woman's face that Lizzy couldn't read. Then she snapped in her default tone, 'Ted Bates ought to mind his own business. He should have better things to do than gossip.'

Lizzy was about to apologise, but the odd look was still on the woman's face, and she stayed silent. May kept her gaze downwards, and Charlie shuffled closer to her.

'If you're done, you'd better come and see't mistress, hadn't you?' the woman dried her hands on her apron. 'If you need to address me, I'm Mrs Gains, the housekeeper. Mr Gains is the groundsman to the estate. But don't thee be mithering me with your chitterling, I've enough to do than have you lot 'round my ankles all the day.'

Mrs Gains took them into the dark corridor beyond the

kitchen. They walked past a cellar door and along to the end of the passageway, stopping at the door Mrs Gains had said belonged to the mistress. She gave a sharp knock and, without waiting for an answer, opened the door. Warm, natural light flooded the dark corridor, pooling around them. The light was so harsh it made them blink.

'These're them, ma'am,' Mrs Gains said it in a loud voice as she walked in, but her tone was much the same as before.

# Chapter 8

The room couldn't be in greater contrast to the rest of the house.

Brocade curtains hung from the leading French window and smaller windows on either side. Sunlight streamed through white net drapes and splashed across the floral pattern of a rich carpet that felt thick underfoot. A fire crackled in the grate, and it flared, making the room too warm, a haven for the palms growing in large pots next to the windows.

Flanked by two Lloyd Loom chairs, an elegant dressing table rested against a wall. A wardrobe in dark polished wood in the same design as the dresser, heavy, stylish, and expensive—stood nearby, and the cloying scent of lavender perfume pervaded the air. Small scent bottles and silver trinket boxes were arranged on the dresser's polished surface, and a large mirror reflected the opulent room.

A variety of paintings and old sepia-brown photographs hung on the walls in a mixture of plain and ornate frames. The images were of people. Relaxed figures leaned against chairs and picnic tables in the less formal photographs. The women wore long dresses with elegant frills, and some even had Victorian bustles. The men were in their shirt-sleeves, slacks, and striped jackets. The figures were posed like the waxwork models Lizzy saw when Susan took them to Madame Tussauds in the formal pictures. Military officers stood to attention dressed in ornate, stately uniforms from another century. Exuding authority, they looked like heroes with their pomp and waxed moustaches.

These were the heirlooms of a bygone age, lost in time when things were different. It was a room of memories, like a museum. The figures reminded Lizzy of the people from an old dolls' house with things you could see but were not allowed to touch.

The large bed faced the French windows and looked so soft and inviting. However, a strange apparition resided there. It was covered in blankets and bright throws grabbing Lizzy's attention.

An old woman, grey and wrinkled, lay prone and still, propped up with pillows and pale as a ghastly phantom. Her white nightdress accentuated the fanciful notion of somebody long dead. The ivory skin looked as thin as paper and clung to her bony face and palsied hands, with prominent blue veins. Jewelled rings adorned skeletal fingers on hands where the knuckles were gnarled with arthritis; the fingers of one hand had curled like a claw. Her cheeks were sunken, and it gave her face a hollow look with watery eyes that were fixed and unblinking. Like the beam of a searchlight, they caught the children and held them in a steady gaze. She scrutinised them intently for what seemed like an age, and her cracked lips grew tighter until they formed a sharp line.

'I am Miss Inglestone,' she said in a thin, reedy warble. 'That will be all, Ede.' This time, her voice was assertive and belied her frailty. She looked at Mrs Gains by the door.

'Ma'am.' Mrs Gains left the room, shutting the door behind her.

'You are Elizabeth, I should think,' Miss Inglestone said to Lizzy. 'The eldest.'

She nodded as she spoke, and before Lizzy could answer, her gaze fell on Charlie.

'Charles,' she gave the same nod.

Then her eyes fell on May.

'Munch. A curious nickname. Or should I call you May? Come closer. These eyes are not as good as they were.'

Lizzy stepped forward hesitantly. Charlie and May edged closer and hid slightly behind their sister, nervous of the ghostly figure in front of them. Feeling like naughty children, they were summoned to see the headmistress.

Miss Inglestone surveyed each child individually, and she nodded as before.

'I was young once. But now I am trapped in this ghastly body. I ask it to do something, and it refuses.' She lifted an arm and let it drop. 'See?'

If it was a question, they didn't dare answer it.

In his nervousness, Charlie looked around rather than at Miss Inglestone. His eyes grazed the walls but couldn't rest on anything for longer than a second.

'Do not get old,' Miss Inglestone commanded. 'I am Eighty-five. Some would call it a good age—a good innings, as they say up here.'

'You don't look Eighty-five.' Lizzy felt she had to say something under the glare of the searchlight.

The woman laughed softly.

'That is clearly a lie, child. However, it is a good lie. But I do and more. That is my father.'

She was old, but her wits were keen, and, despite the remark about her eyes, she was observant. Charlie was looking at a photograph in a polished gilt frame of a distinguished old gentleman. Perhaps in his seventies, the man wore a frock suit, a top hat, and had a cane under his arm. His stare was intense and assured. But Miss Inglestone's words were so sharp that Charlie stared at his shoes and shuffled a bit.

'Old Mr Inglestone. Just as I am Old Miss Inglestone.'

Lizzy's forehead crinkled considering her words, and the woman shifted her attention back to the eldest.

'I'm the last of the Inglestones.'

Lizzy didn't know how to answer and mimicked her brother by shuffling from one foot to the other.

'Do you need the lavatory, child? Do stand still. The last.' she repeated.

She picked up a photograph from the bedside table. It showed a woman and a man in a white suit. Miss Inglestone smiled. It was a sad inward smile meant only for its owner. Miss Inglestone was quiet as if her old thoughts consumed her attention. She seemed to be somewhere else, and her eyes closed as if she was listening to something only she could hear.

Lizzy had seen the same look on her grandmother's face before she passed away—it was an empty vacancy belying a memory. For a moment, she wondered if they should go. May tugged Lizzy's dress wanting to leave, and Lizzy shook her head.

Desperate to break the silence, Lizzy said, 'Thank you for taking us in, Miss Inglestone.' In the quiet room, her voice seemed unusually loud.

Miss Inglestone's eyes opened. It took her a few seconds to focus, and in the thick hush, with only the crackling of the fire breaking the silence, she looked at the children.

'You came highly recommended,' she said in her slow and deliberate way.

'Oh, Mum's friend,' Lizzy was relieved to think they had something they could discuss. 'Auntie Marie must have spoken to you about us.'

'I do not know this Marie, you speak of. You came recommended—enough. Come, take me outside. These sunny days will be few now that winter is here. I want to know if there is any warmth in the sun today.'

Miss Inglestone rose with such effort that Lizzy rushed to help, only to be pushed away. She called her back when she was upright and leaning on a walking stick. Stooped and ungainly, Miss Inglestone made slow progress to the French window. Charlie and May ran to open them and then followed behind her at a respectable distance. They were glad to have something to do away from the old woman's stare.

# Chapter 9

There was no warmth on such an icy day, and Miss Inglestone wrapped herself against the cold. In the acid glare of the sun, she looked paler than before. Her skin was like powdered ash, and her frame was as thin as a stick inside a tight white tube. She looked so frail, a wisp of smoke only that a slight breeze could blow away.

'The end of days,' she muttered. She flicked her head. 'That is Inglestone Manor. But, like me, it has seen better days.' She drew herself upright and held her frame tall, the epitome of grace and elegance.

A few hundred yards away in the near distance, the hulk of a gothic mansion loomed against the skyline. The building Lizzy had glimpsed the night before looked stately. But it was far from that. It was dark and foreboding, even in the sunlight. The windows were all broken, and the light glimmered off the splintered glass. There was a black emptiness beyond the recess of each window. The building's facade was covered in moss, and even that looked sickly. Some of its once magnificent chimneys had collapsed, leaving a silhouette like broken teeth against the sky. The neglected house had the appearance of being hollow. Great malice had befallen it, and she'd been ravaged by fire. The blackened beams, the ribs of the house, rose above the shattered walls and caved-in roof. The fire had consumed one of its great wings and damaged the rest of the building. It was left like a shipwreck, washed up on the dark moors, and the thick grass swaying in the wind lapped like the ocean waves around it.

Leading up to the mansion, a path had long ago yielded to the wiles of nature and was patched with grass and small bushes that pushed through the dark gravel. A red brick wall surrounded the ruin, and it too lay broken, the bricks piled up in heaps of abandoned masonry. The iron gate and its gatehouse were gone, and only the gap remained, framed by two black posts to tell it was ever there. A gaping hole was the only indication that there must have been a gate of imposing size.

'That is where I was born,' Miss Inglestone said. She lifted her head with a proud arrogance. 'Once, it was grand. But times change, and things move on. Time is never a kind bedfellow. When I go, it will go also. It will be torn down, and people shall forget it was ever there. Just as they will forget about the Inglestones. I am the last of them, Elizabeth Allen. There is none left to carry on. It is not a bad thing. As they say, we have had a good run— we have had our day.'

She looked at the children in turn. Above them, Mrs Gains stared down from a top window. When Miss Inglestone followed Charlie's gaze to the housekeeper, their eyes met.

'It still has secrets,' Miss Inglestone said.

'Secrets?' Lizzy said.

Miss Inglestone nodded.

'All houses have secrets, Elizabeth Allen. The older they are, the more they have. The first brick of that old lady was laid in the seventeenth century. And it has been built upon and extended since. It has many secrets.'

There was a grace about her. She was old and frail, but there was still a stubborn strength inside the old woman.

'The Inglestones are an old family. Sons and fathers have fought and died for their country; there have been sad times and happy ones. We have entertained the great, the good, the not-so-great, and the not-so-good. And the terrible fire has done for the place. It has been in decline ever since, a victim to the ravages of time and nature. All that remains of her is this lodge.'

She leant against Lizzy as she stared at the crumbling building. However, Lizzy barely felt the weight.

'It is an odd place now. Someone is inside, I think. At night, there are strange lights. I see them sometimes before bed. Ghosts from the past wander its corridors, searching for a way out. They remember a party or a dance from long ago. I know it because I hear the music on the wind, the strain of old melodies. If you listen, so will you.'

Her voice was dreamy and quiet.

'They say it is my imagination. Doolally, I believe, is the expression they use. Poppycock, I'm as sane as the next person.'

Remembering the plump lady's words at the railway station, Lizzy didn't know what to say, so she didn't say anything.

'It is not a place to be alone anymore. Inglestone Manor will keep its secrets—no matter what.'

'What secrets has it got?' May asked.

Miss Inglestone looked at the girl. The sun softened her eyes and made her a different person from the apparition festering in the bedroom.

'Is there treasure?' May, sounded hopeful.

'Hush. May,' Lizzy was alarmed at the forwardness of her sister and remembered Mrs Gains's reaction when asked that question.

Miss Inglestone gave a thin laugh and raised a hand to silence Lizzy. It was strange hearing her laughter, a much younger sound from so gaunt a woman.

'And what if I said there is?' She asked May as if teasing her.

May shrugged awkwardly.

'Would you try and find it?'

The little girl flushed.

'Many have, Munch. Some still do,' she whispered.

As May looked at the manor in awe, a sparkle lit the old lady's eyes.

'Some things are lost forever and can never be found. Do you believe that, May Allen?'

Unused to such questions, May was silent.

'I thought I did once,' Miss Inglestone said.

Lizzy knew she wasn't speaking to May or to anyone else. And when the woman readjusted her gaze, it was to the ruin again, and Lizzy could only wonder what she saw there.

'You mind the cold, ma'am,' Mrs Gains said from the

open window. 'The doctor says it's dangerous at your age. Better come inside, now. It's a bit fresh today.'

'My jailer,' she mumbled to Lizzy. 'At my age, living is dangerous, Ede,' she shouted, without looking up at Mrs Gains.

'Aye, ma'am. If you say so.'

# Chapter 10

The children spent the rest of the day wandering around the house and garden. They went down the lane towards the village, kicking stones along the way. They never went far enough to be out of sight of the lodge. They saw Mr Gains a few times; they watched as he crossed the fields, coming from the direction of the manor. He was dressed in the same clothes as the night before and carried a shotgun in the crook of his arm. Lizzy wondered if he had another dead rabbit somewhere in his coat. She hoped he wouldn't produce it like a magician, just before supper.

He had a snarling Alsatian keeping time with him; Mr Gains clutched the chain around the animal's neck. The dog strained against it, growling and pulling him along. Lizzy thought it was an unusual dog to have, remembering what her father said about farm dogs— good hunting dogs, he said, have soft mouths.

The next time they saw Mr Gains, they'd wandered to the broken brick wall surrounding the manor. He was walking on the gravel drive between the missing gates, and the dog ran free in front of him. It barked at everything and sniffed the ground and bushes. As they watched, Mr Gains went along the perimeter of the manor towards the fire-razed wing, shouting to the dog, 'Here, Sabre. Come here.' The dog's ears pricked, and he bounded over to his master.

Lizzy thought about a plan of action—a term she'd heard her mother use. "We need a plan of action for when the holidays come, Susan. Otherwise, there'll be chaos."

Top of the list was exploring, though it was more a case of getting out of the depressing lodge and away from Mrs Gains. There was a spark of curiosity there, and she wasn't sure if it was a good spark. She remembered the housekeeper's expression after they had seen Miss Inglestone. She knew for sure that wasn't good.

They planned to visit the village for a shufti, Susan's word for having a look. Lizzy said they'd venture further and explore the outskirts when they knew more. But they had to go back to the lodge because it was almost dinnertime. Mrs Gains had warned them about being late, saying, 'We are punctual for mealtimes. I've better things to do than wait on you lot. There'll be nowt to eat 'till supper if you're late.'

Lizzy was sure she meant it.

Dinner was a small meal, satisfying and tasty. Mrs Gains put the plates beside them in the same rough manner as the previous night and, in her busy way, she disappeared with her broom and dustpan. Anxious about her coming back, they ate quickly, finishing everything they'd been given. When Mrs Gains returned, she said, 'Well, there's no time like the present, is there? Sink's over there. Stack plates on't side when you're done,' and then she bustled off to another part of the house.

Lizzy gathered the plates and washed them. When Mrs Gains saw the stacked plates, she made a huffing noise. She did everything loud as if she was making a point about how busy she was and expected their work to be wrong or not done at all. She put the broom and pan in the kitchen corner with a clatter and bang.

'I'm going to the village. I need your ration cards.'

Lizzy went to get them, leaving Charlie and May.

They looked at their feet, wanting to be invisible and unnoticed.

Mrs Gains put her coat on and clutched a wicker basket in her hand. Lizzy handed over the cards, and she put them in her pocket without looking at them.

'You mustn't lose them. They're important,' Charlie

said.

'What did you say, boy? Do you think I lose things?'

Charlie squirmed and averted his eyes from Mrs Gains's icy stare.

'No, Mrs Gains,' Lizzy said quickly, 'Charlie didn't mean that. Our maid said to look after them, that's all.'

'Maid? I'm not your bloomin' maid, you toffs, just remember that. I should have bloody known you'd have maids.'

She glowered at Charlie.

'I'm sorry, Mrs Gains,' Charlie said timidly.

'The biddy's asleep. If she wakes, she'll call.'

She tied her headscarf and left, muttering to herself as she went. They watched her march toward the village at a stomping pace that Lizzy thought she could maintain, there and back.

Charlie looked dejected. He looked as though he wanted to say something, but the words choked in his mouth.

'Come on, cheer up—she's gone,' Lizzy said.

'I know—but Susan said not to let anybody get hold of our ration cards.'

'I know. But best not mention Susan in front of Mrs

Gains again. Okay?'

Lizzy was getting the measure of Mrs Gains and how different things were here.

'What's a toff, Lizzy? Are we toffs?' May asked.

'It's just a rude word, Munch. No, we're not toffs.'

# Chapter 11

That evening, as they sat down to supper, Bill Gains came in, dirtier and more dishevelled than usual. He was in a foul temper and glowered at the children as he entered the kitchen. He looked as if he'd taken a tumble. His coat and trousers were muddy on one side, and his face was streaked with caked-on mud. Mrs Gains asked him what happened, and he mumbled a swear word, too angry to speak. He flung his coat at her and put the shotgun on the hook before storming out of the kitchen towards the bathroom. She followed. There was an exchange in the corridor that the children couldn't make out. The tone was harsh and angry. Mrs Gains got a stiff brush and went brisk and bustling outside.

The children swapped glances and sniggered.

'What was that about?' Charlie whispered.

Lizzy shook her head. 'He didn't half look funny.'

'Maybe he had a fight?' May said.

'He must have lost,' Charlie said.

They giggled at the thought.

They had stew for supper, and when Lizzy tasted it, she knew it was rabbit stew. Her eyes darted to Charlie and May, remembering the dead animal on the counter and what Mrs Gains said about the game being plenty.

'My, this chicken tastes good, but it's a bit different—it must be the way they cook it here. I reckon it's the sauce; it's a much stronger flavour than Mum's, that's for sure.'

She needn't have worried. Charlie and May were hungry and tucked in, agreeing that the chicken did taste funny.

By the time they'd finished, Mrs Gains had come in. The coat was brushed clean of mud, and she hung it on a hook beside the gun. She busied herself in the kitchen, moving things from one place to another—and often back again. When she saw they'd finished, she motioned to the sink. After collecting the dishes, Lizzy washed and rinsed them while Charlie dried. May didn't want to be alone on the remote island that was the table, so she stood with them as they worked.

When Mr Gains came back from the bathroom, his face and hands were spotless. He'd changed into fresh clothes, and he handed his trousers to his wife, who took up the stiff brush and went outside again, followed by her husband.

'Well, what happened?' they heard her say.

Lizzy cleared away the salt and pepper pots and collected the mats. She did it slowly, trying to listen to their conversation.

'Little beggar,' Mr Gains snapped. 'I nearly had him. Sabre sniffed him out and went for him.'

Mrs Gains brushed the mud from the trousers with quick strokes.

'The boy?' she said. 'Ted was saying that some's escaped again. So he's back, is he? Where this time?'

'Where do you think? In the old ballroom, where else?'

Mr Gains lit a cigarette. The match flared and revealed his angry red face. He took a deep drag and exhaled a breath of smoke.

'Here, you didn't have a shot at him?'

'Why? Do you think anyone would care? Sabre chased him and then lost him, that's all.'

'He knows that manor better than you do, Billy.'

'Sod that. I was so close, Ede, so bloomin' close to getting him I was.'

'Next time, maybe—but he ain't worth swinging for.'

Mrs Gains shook the trousers hard and held them up to

the light streaming through the open kitchen door. Satisfied that they were clean, she folded them across her arm. Bill gave her a look and smoked his cigarette in silence.

'You sure it was him, the same boy?'

'Oh, aye, it was him, alright. Couldn't be anyone else.'

'Do you think he's got it?'

'I don't know. But if he has, he'll regret it.'

'Come on, I'll get you some supper. There'll be another time.'

She saw Lizzy hovering by the kitchen table, holding the salt and pepper pot.

'You heard enough, Miss Nose?'

Lizzy jumped and went red with embarrassment.

'We mind our own business around here,' Mr Gains said.

'Just you remember that missy,' his wife said.

Lizzy was going to deny that she'd been eavesdropping. However, she froze, unused to such intrigues, she couldn't think of anything to say.

'Aye, you'll get the back of me hand if you forget.' Mr Gains frowned. Something angry lurked in his eyes, and he didn't try to hide it.

'I think it's bedtime,' Mrs Gains said. 'The old biddy'll want to see you lot before you go up. You can take her milk when you do.'

The children hung around as Mrs Gains warmed a pan of milk. Lizzy felt Mr Gains's icy stare on her, making the silence thick and uncomfortable.

# Chapter 12

Dorothy Inglestone was reading in bed when Lizzy tapped on her door. At her bidding, the children entered and felt out of place. They stood nervously at the bottom of her bed. The warm smile from the old lady soon put them at ease. She seemed changed, or at least that was Lizzy's impression.

She inquired about their day and patted the bed for them to sit.

Old Miss Inglestone had an easy way with people. At first, the children were hesitant and gave short answers to her questions. But after some comments about how pretty they looked, and what a good reply that was, they felt comfortable, and soon they were laughing with her.

'I do not receive many guests these days. The Gains are not good company. Only my doctor calls, and he keeps prescribing me those awful pills. And the occasional visitor—namely the priest—comes to visit. I think he is planning my funeral.'

Her words brought a nervous laugh from the Allens.

Miss Inglestone leant forward and whispered into May's ear loud enough so they could all hear. 'He will be disappointed, I assure you. My intention is to go kicking and screaming when the hearse arrives.' She gave May a wink.

May's hand came up to cover her mouth, and she gaped in surprise.

'Oh May, you remind me of myself when I was your age,' Miss Inglestone sounded happy.

She took May's hand. For a moment, she was quiet, deep in thought. When she opened her eyes, Lizzy was looking at the photograph on the bedside table. A young woman leaned against a handsome, moustached man dressed in a white suit in the faded black and white image. There was a happy informality in their pose. The old lady picked up the photograph and ran a wrinkled finger across the face of the man.

'That is Carlos,' she said, showing them the photograph. 'Carlos Louis Rodriguez. My *amante*. And that is I. You see, I was young once too, Elizabeth Allen.'

Lizzy blushed while the others giggled. She didn't mean to pry so openly, especially after being caught eavesdropping by Mrs Gains.

'We lived in a villa in a suburb of Buenos Aires. That is in South America, in a country called Argentina. It was a beautiful white house that overlooked the river. Oh, what times we had.'

Her eyes sparkled, and she gave Lizzy a conspiratorial smile.

'He was a politician. Every day was exciting. I felt so alive then like I had never felt before or since—I do not mind admitting that I would not have traded a single minute of it.'

Lizzy warmed to her. There was pride in her voice. She was comfortable and open and not the ghostly apparition they met. She'd changed in such a short time just by having company.

'So, you ask, what am I doing here?' Miss Inglestone closed her eyes as if in pain and then sighed. The smile left her mouth. 'Alas, all things come to an end. I have come home to die.' She said it matter-of-factly.

'Miss Inglestone,' Lizzy was shocked, and Charlie and May stared open-mouthed.

'I have had a good life. I have no complaints,' Miss Inglestone said brightly. 'I was left more than enough money to last me, and I had everything I wanted. There is just one last thing to do, and that is being done. I'm fulfilling my father's wishes.'

'Your father's wishes?' Lizzy caught herself. 'I'm sorry, Miss Inglestone, I didn't mean to pry.'

If Miss Inglestone was offended, she did not show it.

'I have a promise to keep. One I made a long time ago. I confess that I do not understand it all yet. But promises are made to be kept. Now, Katherine May Allen, I have a present for you.'

May looked at her curiously and then at her brother and sister.

The old lady rummaged through a drawer of the bedside cabinet. She pulled May towards her when she found what she was looking for. Hampered by arthritis, her hands trembled as she fixed a small pin on the girl's chest. It was the figure of a prancing hare. The brooch was made of gold and less than an inch long, with a tiny ruby for its eye.

'There, doesn't that look good? It was my grandmother's. She gave it to me on my ninth birthday. I got a doll and a book and all kinds of nice things. But of all the presents that day, this was my favourite. I wore it the first time I met Carlos, and I felt it brought me luck. It will bring you luck as well, May. I know it.'

May blushed and smiled. When Lizzy gave her a

gentle push, she said, 'Thank you, Miss Inglestone.'

'It is my pleasure. It is not an overly expensive thing, but it is of great sentiment. As one grows older, sentiment is the only thing left that is of real value.'

Miss Inglestone closed her eyes and said, 'goodnight, children.'

The day ended happily, something Lizzy was grateful for. Together in the double bed and under the light of a candle, she read them a chapter from *War and Peace*. It was a cosy reminder of their home in London.

As she read, Lizzy knew that May wasn't listening. Her sister's gaze was fixed on the golden hare with the ruby eye. When May had changed for bed, she made sure her jumper was the last thing placed on the back of the chair, with the hare on top. It would be the first thing she saw when she got up.

# Chapter 13

The next day dawned bright and cold. Lizzy went to say good morning to Miss Inglestone before breakfast while May and Charlie tidied the bedroom. Breakfast was a silent affair, especially under the cold eyes of Mrs Gains. The pecking sarcasm in her voice made it a welcome relief when they left the lodge and wandered along the path to the village.

In the distance, they saw a hotchpotch of grey slate roofs and gently smoking chimneys. The church spire ascended to a singular sharp point at the centre of what was more a town than a village. A lazy river flowed in a broad meander across the open ground beyond the houses. On the arrow-straight railway embankment, a train puffed along. A plume of thick grey smoke erupted from its black funnel as it drew into the station. The echoing clack of wheels and the sharp whistle were the only sounds in the air that floated the smoke in a languid sky.

They strolled along the empty morning streets of the village, looking in shop windows as they passed. There was a bric-a-brac shop, a small café, and a newsagent. On a stone bridge, they lingered awhile, throwing pebbles into the swirling waters of an icy stream, before walking along the bank. Some children were playing football across the river. They watched them until a goal was scored before going back into town. May had acquired a stick, and she flicked the ground with it as she walked.

Their conversation had centred on old Miss Inglestone and her South American lover. Lizzy commented that she looked so young, remembering the image of the girl in the bedside photograph.

'Miss Inglestone had two sisters. She told me this morning. They both died before she was ten. There was a brother as well, who died in India where he was a soldier. It's very sad—too sad to dwell upon, she said. Her mother suffered a long illness brought on by grief, and she died just before the last war started. Then, Miss Inglestone's father died in a fire. So she's the only one left of her entire family. Can you imagine that?'

'What did she mean when she said she's come home to die?' Charlie asked.

'I guess she wants to die here, where she was born, rather than in Buenos Aires.'

'Do you think she sent for us, Lizzy? Like the

policeman said. I mean, she doesn't know us, does she? We haven't met her before. And she called May, Munch like we do. How does she know that?'

'I don't know Charlie, but I was curious about that, too. I thought it was a bit strange. Maybe Mum or Auntie Marie told her about us.'

'But she said she didn't know Aunt Marie.'

'She did, didn't she? But the policeman and the lady said she'd asked for us especially.' Lizzy couldn't make sense of it.

'Maybe we remind her of her family? She said how alike she and Munch are.'

'And she said something about making a promise to her father,' May said, jumping in on the conversation for the first time.

Lizzy looked perplexed. 'I think she's just lonely. I mean, Mr and Mrs Gains aren't much company. And Mum would have told us if she knew her. Mum said she'd made arrangements, and Miss Inglestone was doing us a favour.'

'But Mum also said she'd asked for us. Maybe mum met her when we were younger.'

'Well, I don't remember her, Charlie,' May aimed a

kick at a stone. 'But no one tells me anything.'

They'd been wandering for hours, and the cold was biting. They were outside the library and went in to escape the chill.

## Chapter 14

It was a small library, just a large room, with shelves and cases of books arranged in neat aisles. A desk to sign books out was near the entrance and out of the draught. The plump lady they met at the railway station when they came to Inglestone, was behind it. This time she wore a bright red cardigan.

'Eh, Missy,' she said, recognising them. She winked and gave May a motherly smile. 'You can't bring weapons in here, luv. Best leave it against the wall, for now, eh, pet?'

May smiled back and leant her stick against a wall.

'Can we have a look around, please?' Lizzy asked.

'Aye, help yourself. If you want to take anything out, you let me know.' Still smiling, she turned towards May. 'You look famished, luv. Here, have a biscuit. I know how much you likes them.'

She opened a drawer and took out a plate with a layer of biscuits. 'The shortbread's nice.'

'Be careful, Miss,' Lizzy said, 'you don't know her; she'll eat the lot if you let her.'

May huffed and pouted at her sister.

'Aye, well, she looks like she could use a feeding. So, you're up from smoke, are you? And staying with the old lady? Eeh, you're a long way from home but safe from German bombs up here, luv. No one's gonna drop bombs here. Nowt worth bombing, you see.'

'But they bombed the house by the lodge where we're staying,' May said, puzzled.

Milly raised her hand to her mouth and laughed, but it was more of a girlish titter.

'Nay, luv. Germans didn't do that. No, burnt down it did years ago. Long before war started.'

'No one ever tells me anything,' May complained, and Milly laughed.

'Then I'll tell you. Them's queer folk in't lodge, aren't they? Them's all queer there. Him and her, that Billy Gains and Ede. And that dotty one. He's still searching, you know.'

'Searching?'

'Aye, I saw the look in your eyes when Ted spoke to him. There's nowt there to find, but he keeps looking does our Billy.'

'Is he looking for treasure?' May asked.

'Aye, treasure! You know he's been looking since he

got the groundsman job, and before that if you listen to what others say. Not that's there anything to grounds keep anymore. The place has gone to rack and ruin. Why it needs a groundsman is anyone's guess. Poacher turned gamekeeper is him.'

She offered May another biscuit, and Lizzy thought the prospect of new visitors to an ill-used library was something Milly couldn't resist. It was a chance to talk— or gossip more likely.

'Aye, treasure. The Inglestone Diamonds is what treasure is.'

May's eyes lit up.

'Eh, luv, that there book, the one on the rack by you— yes, that one with the brown cover. Bring it over here, will you, luv.'

Charlie found the small book in a light brown cloth binding and brought it over. It was titled: *A History of the Inglestone Family*. Milly flicked through the pages until she came to a section with black and white photographs. She turned more pages and found the one she was looking for.

'This is them.'

May and Charlie looked at a faded picture of a stately

woman in her forties. It was one of those stiff, formal portraits taken when photography was the new art form. She was sitting with a man dressed in a morning suit— they recognised him. It was Old Mr Inglestone. The woman was wearing a necklace so large it looked clumsy. It had a fat pendant of a single diamond surrounded by a halo of smaller ones. Her delicate features mirrored those of the old lady in the lodge.

'That's Mrs Inglestone—Old Miss Inglestone's mother. And that's her father. A handsome couple, wouldn't you say, children?'

'Is that the treasure?' May leant towards the image.

'Aye, the Inglestone Diamonds. Lost now some twenty-five years. He went doolally, they say. Completely off his rocker. Eh, you can't blame him. All his children dead, his wife as well, and only one left. Dotty Dorothy, we call her—gallivanting to South America. They reckon her dad hid the diamonds somewhere in the manor and went so off his head that he forgot where he stashed them.'

She laughed and offered more biscuits. This time to Lizzy, who had joined them.

'Anyway, pet, he died before he let on to anyone

where they were. Perished in the fire—1919, I think it were, just after the war. Some says he was murdered.'

'Murdered.' May's mouth opened wide.

'Aye, least that's what they say. He were confronted by a villain that wanted to steal the diamonds, and when he wouldn't hand them over, he was done away with. Then the robber set fire to the manor to hide his crime. Your Billy Gains were there at the time. He was a stable boy—said he seen the bloke wot done it run away. But they never did find him that did it.'

May scrutinised the photographs.

'But the old bloke couldn't remember where he'd hid them, so how could he have told him that was robbing him? Silly so and so. Everyone always said the old man was strange, ever since he was a boy, always disappearing and telling tall stories about travelling here and travelling there. Anyways, Old Mr Inglestone took his secret to the grave.'

'Poor Miss Inglestone. And she's the last of her family, she told us.' Lizzy said.

'Aye, poor her all right. She's poor as a church mouse, now. I feel sorry for her, having no one to leave anything to, not that she's got anything now anyways. She still owns the manor—but that's not worth owning. The place is more falling down than standing. She comes back before the war. I mean, South America might be a nice place and all, but there's nothing like being home, is there? The only good thing is when she goes, them will have to go as well.'

'Do you mean the Gains?' Lizzy asked.

'Aye, and good riddance to bad rubbish, I say. That Billy's a wrong 'un. Been so all his life. Ever since he was a bairn—pulls the wings off flies, that one. As for the other one, well.' She huffed. 'Aye, and the manor will be pulled down and the lodge sold, and that'll be that.'

There was a swell of noise from the street. Milly paused in her narrative, got up and stood by the entrance.

# Chapter 15

Some scruffy German prisoners of war marched in an untidy line through the village square. Most of them were elderly, except for two in their late teens. They marched happily, smoking and laughing and seemed unconcerned about their status. Some carried hoes and spades that they shouldered like rifles. A few old British soldiers shepherded the prisoners, but it was a half-hearted procession. They would go to a farm or dig a ditch somewhere, and they all chatted like allies.

A group of village boys followed, shouting abuse, gawping and singing a rude song about Hitler. The prisoners ignored the taunts. When they didn't get a reaction, some of the boys threw stones at them.

One of the German lads shouted for them to go away in broken English, only to receive a barrage of derision. One of the village boys shouted, *'Sieg Heil!'* and raised his arm in a Nazi salute. He put two fingers of his other hand under his nose, like a moustache. It was taken up by the rest, who chanted, *'Sieg Heil! Sieg Heil! Sieg Heil!'*

Ted, the policeman, came up behind the boys and gave the biggest one a hard slap across his head. It made a resounding thump, and the boy fled with his friends in tow.

'I know you, Danny Barker. Next time I see you, you'll get more than the back of my hand. You hear me, Danny Barker?'

Danny Barker didn't care to reply.

Milly shook her head and came back inside the library. She looked at the children with sad eyes.

'This war brings out the worst in us, don't it? Them Germans are only trying to help. They just want all this done with, like us. They work on the farms and some at the Asylum up the hill—Holcombe House them call it. Now, there's a thankless job, looking after them queer folks up there, poor devils. I mean, someone has to look after them, don't they? Not me, wouldn't do for me with all that muck and screaming.'

'How queer are they?' Lizzy asked.

'They're loonies. Sorry, love, I mean lunatics. You know, mad people. Oh, don't you worry, pet, even when one gets out, they're not dangerous, never mind what some says.'

'Get out? You mean they can escape?'

'Sometimes one will run away and hide and do

something silly—but only silly mind. Aye, they do that every now and then.'

'I hope they catch them when they do.'

'Oh, they do. But it breaks your heart, it does. Some are so young, your age even, and if you met them on the street, you'd not know different—they look just like you and me. Just a while back, a boy and his two mates ran away. And the things they do to them. It's to cure them, they say. Cure them. Poor souls. More like torture them.'

'What do you mean?'

'They electrocute them. With electricity like.'

Lizzy flinched, and May and Charlie's mouths dropped open.

'I worked there once. Never again. It's not right, hooking them up to an electric cable and running a current through them.'

'That's horrible,' Lizzy said.

'Aye, Electroshock therapy, they call it. Torture, I say. I heard them scream, I did. It were torture. No more, no less. Electroshock therapy, indeed. No wonder they run away. I would if I were them. And I'd never go back.'

Lizzy swallowed. May and Charlie's eyes had grown wide as they stared at her. Seeing them so shocked, the lady giggled, realising she had been rambling an awful story in front of children.

'Oh, luv, I'm sorry, I didn't mean to frighten you. It's just that it's not right hurting them like that.'

Much to her relief, Ted came into the library. He shook his head with a cross look on his face.

'Just wait until I get my hands on Danny Barker. I'll give him a thick ear, the trouble maker.'

'He needs his father to keep him in line.'

'Aye. Unfortunately, you can't just jump on a train from Burma, much the pity.'

'And speaking of trouble, what happened last night? I heard such a commotion before bed. I thought it were a riot.'

'You heard that, did you? That were Billy Gains, drunk as a lord and spending like a sailor. Got into a fight with the landlord. "Get on your way, Billy," says Davey. "You're cut and rude, and I ain't serving you again tonight."

'And Billy says, "Me money's as good as anyone else's," and he slaps five pounds—Aye! Five pounds— slaps it on't counter and demands another beer. Well, Davey's not gonna stand for that, is he? and squares up to him. An' who gets called out from his warm cot to sort out the mess. Me, that's who. Davey says he was acting the fool and flush with cash.'

'Five pounds? I didn't know Billy got paid that much.'

'It's Billy Gains, Milly.' Pursing his lips, Ted clucked rudely.

She laughed and took a biscuit, nibbling at the corner.

When Ted saw the children, he stood with his hands on his hips, leant back, and gave them a broad smile.

'Well, what have we here? These are the pups, are they? Looking a lot better than when I last seen them. Bright and cheery—if I may say so. So, how's the lodge? Are you enjoying your stay?'

Lizzy gave a sheepish smile and said, 'Yes, sir, we're comfortable. It's a nice place. The food's nice. And we're safe.'

Ted broke out into a hearty laugh.

'Well, there's faint praise indeed, don't you think, Milly? Well, them Gains aren't pretty people, that's for sure. But you landed on your feet with old Miss Inglestone. She's a right one. Game for anything. I knew her when she was young. She were this beautiful vision, but that were before she left for foreign parts.'

'He was in love with her,' Milly teased, giving the Allens a wink.

'Eh, it would have been easy to fall for that one. I were only a young 'un myself.'

'Was she pretty?' May asked.

'Pretty as a picture she were—almost as pretty as you. Turned many a young men's heads. And kind. That were the other thing about her—she was kind. That's why she'll do good by you.'

He told them about her and what a grand place the manor was, especially with all the parties. The children were enthralled and listened intently.

'Christmas was a good time back then. There were carriages up to the drive. Old ones, I mean, horse-pulled ones. No motorcars back then. The manor looked like one of them picture postcards when the snow fell. You should have seen it, magical it was, mark my word. Magical. Aye, times have changed.'

'Did you ever see the treasure?' May asked.

'Treasure, lass?'

'She means the Inglestone Jewels, Ted—she were all ears back at the railway station.' Milly placed a hand on May's shoulder. 'That's all this one ever talks about, treasure this and treasure that.'

'Now, what is it you've been telling them, woman? Gossiping again?'

'No more than what they should know. You know as well as I do how that Billy Gains's been looking for the diamonds these past twenty years. And what's he found? Nowt. That's what. Nowt.' She turned to Lizzy. 'Myself, I reckon old Mr Inglestone lost them gambling. They all say he was one for the ponies. I mean, look at the place? He'd have put it right for his daughter if he had any money, wouldn't he? No, love, trust me, he lost it gambling and was too proud to admit losing the family fortune. I mean, how stupid can you get?'

Lizzy was too well brought up to question the lady as to whether Mr Inglestone had hid the diamonds or gambled them away, so she kept quiet. And Milly was so engrossed and happy with the company that she didn't want to spoil it for her.

Ted shook his head.

'Old Mr Inglestone was a very clever man, Milly, not that you'd know. You were too young to remember.'

'But you did see the jewels, didn't you, Ted?' Milly said.

'Aye. One Christmas, as it happens. She were wearing them, the mother, I mean.' The book was open at the photograph. 'That's her, and that's them. She looks grand, doesn't she? Aye. I remember that like it were yesterday. Good times.'

'We thought we'd look inside the manor.' Lizzy was enjoying the policeman's company.

'We're going to find the treasure,' May said enthusiastically.

'Eh, now,' Ted said. His face was serious, and he narrowed his eyes to make his point. 'You pups best take care. That place is dangerous. Ain't no one lived there nigh on thirty-year. The place is falling down. Walk around outside if you want but take heed, and don't go inside. I'm sure the floors will be weak, and you might fall through and hurt yourselves. It's a big place, is the manor, and we don't want you getting lost inside. It's big enough to swallow you up, and we'll never find you all again.'

'Miss Inglestone said she's seen people inside,' Charlie said.

'No, lad, no one's there.'

'But she did. She said that parties are going on at

night.'

The policeman and the plump lady laughed.

'Poor woman, she remembers the past,' he said. 'When you're as old as she, things like that happen. Old-timers disease, they calls it. Her mind's wandering. That's all there is to it.'

'She's remembering a party she went to when she were young,' Milly said. 'The mind plays tricks when you get older, but not half as much tricks as the wind. The wind makes strange sounds at night, especially when it blows across moors. It can sound like voices, it can. Like a ventriloquist dummy—you don't know where the sounds coming from. And the poor dear's getting on, and she don't know the difference.'

'Mr Gains said he chased a boy there—maybe that's what she heard,' Charlie said.

'Probably one of the boys from the village,' Ted said. 'I see I'll have to have a word with them about playing there again. I can see that now the school's out. The place is a death trap, but it's a fairground for them.'

The clock struck the quarter, a short, sharp, piercing chime.

'Ay-Up. Duty calls, no rest for the wicked,' the

policeman said. 'Now you lot take care not to go inside that old manor. We don't get much excitement 'round 'ere, which is just how we like it.'

Seeing the time, Lizzy said they had to go, but Charlie asked to borrow the book before they left.

'We're going to have to run.' Lizzy was worried about being late for lunch, and they set off at a quick trot to the lodge.

# Chapter 16

It had been a good day, and Lizzy was content and happy. On their way back to the lodge, however, they passed Holcombe House, and Lizzy gave it a hard stare, imagining the awful cures that went on there. She didn't mention where they were as they ran past. Neither Charlie nor May needed reminding what Milly said.

That evening, they sat in bed with thoughts of Holcombe House forgotten. They drew the blankets around them to ward off the cold, and Charlie read from the library book.

'It says here that... *"The Inglestone Diamonds are made up of a fifty-carat red diamond in a pendant surrounded by one-carat red diamonds. The rings and earrings are between two and three-carat and mounted on a 22-carat gold base."* And that the brooch is the same, apparently, containing a mixture of between two and three-carat diamonds.'

May looked puzzled. 'How come diamonds are made of carrots, Lizzy?'

Charlie sniggered at her, and May pouted. 'Carats, Ca-rats, not Car-rots, stupid. You can't eat them.'

'I'm not stupid.' May snapped. 'I'm not, Mr La-de-da,' and she drew her legs up, folding her arms in a sulk.

Lizzy's brow furrowed the way their mother's did when she was displeased.

Charlie saw Lizzy's annoyed face and sighed, 'Sorry, Munch. I didn't mean it. Honestly, you're not stupid at all. I'm stupid for calling you stupid, which was stupid.'

May refused to be pacified.

'It's how they weigh diamonds, Munch,' Lizzy explained. 'They call it a carat. A one-carat diamond is pretty big—it's bigger than the one on Mummy's ring. So, a fifty-carat diamond is huge.'

'No one ever tells me anything,' May mumbled.

'And look how many there are.' Lizzy showed her the photograph.

May glanced up but tried to look as though she wasn't interested.

'Are they really red?' She looked at the black and white pictures.

Lizzy shrugged. She knew how diamonds were weighed, but she'd assumed they were always transparent colourless crystals.

This time, Charlie spoke directly to May, 'It says, red

diamonds are very rare. So, they must be even more expensive and probably worth thousands.'

'Millions and millions.' May said, looking at the picture. 'Look how many there are. Is that what old Mr Inglestone hid?'

'Or gambled away. I wonder why he did it. He could have given them to Miss Inglestone. She was his daughter. The library lady said she's as poor as a church mouse now,' Lizzy said.

For a while, they speculated on old Mr Inglestone's motives. Much of it was fanciful, but it was getting late. Lizzy suggested they read another chapter of War and Peace and go to sleep.

When Lizzy finished the chapter, she put the book in the bedside drawer. She kept it out of sight because Mrs Gains's accusation about them being toffs had hurt her feelings. They weren't rich or upper-class, even if they did have a maid. But a smart book like that would only confirm Mrs Gains's opinion. When she opened the drawer, she noticed that her purse was open. When she looked inside, it was empty. She tried to remember when she last looked in it.

'Charlie, when you made the beds this morning, can

you remember if my purse was open?'

Charlie shook his head and saw the serious look on his sister's face.

'May, do you remember?' Lizzy asked.

May also shook her head.

'What's wrong?' Charlie asked.

'Mummy's money's gone,' Lizzy said in a trembling voice.

'What money?'

'It was there when I put it away when we arrived. I'm sure it was.'

'Lizzy, what money?' Charlie asked again.

'When you and May were asleep on the train, I took one five-pound note and put it in my coat, and that first night, I put it in the back of the book. I wanted to keep one safe in case of emergencies.' She opened the book towards the back, and the five-pound note was tucked in against the spine. 'I left the other one in my purse.'

'Ten pounds?' Charlie said, 'Where did you get ten pounds?'

'Somebody's taken it.'

'Lizzy, where did you get ten pounds?' Charlie asked.

'Mum gave it to me before we left—she said it was for

treats and things. I can't have lost it, I can't. It was here, I swear, it was here.' She held up her empty purse.

'Maybe it fell out on the train,' May said.

'No, it didn't. I know it didn't.'

Lizzy rummaged through the drawer in a panic. Taking out its meagre contents, she peered inside and looked in the drawer below and then around the floor, her eyes watered up.

'I had it. I can't have lost it.'

'Maybe someone stole it on the train when we were asleep?' Charlie said.

Lizzy found her suitcase and looked inside, turning it upside down and giving it a shake. But nothing fell out. She sat on the bed, looking blankly at the floor as though it would magically appear. When it dawned on her that the money was gone, she cried, whispering that she couldn't have lost it when Mum had trusted her to look after it? Her body heaved as she sobbed.

May was first up. She climbed onto her sister's bed and wrapped her arms around Lizzy. She placed the side of her face against her shoulder. Charlie hugged her too.

'We still have one left,' May said through her own sniffles.

Lizzy managed a weak smile as she looked at the five-pound note.

'Yes. We still have one left. And I don't want any treats anyways,' Charlie said.

'Me neither,' May said. She looked stoic and shook her head defiantly.

Lizzy sniffed back her tears and wiped a sleeve across her running nose. She mumbled that they should get some sleep. Charlie and May slipped into their bed, and Lizzy tucked them in so that they were snug.

'The troop's all present and correct, corporal Elizabeth,' Charlie said with a salute.

A weak smile edged Lizzy's mouth, 'All present and correct, private Charles.'

Lizzy got into bed, blew out the candle, and closed her eyes. But sleep eluded her, and she played over in her mind what could have happened on the train. At least May was right, they had one left, and she was determined to not lose it.

# Chapter 17

In the morning, the lost money played on Lizzy's mind, and throughout breakfast, she was quiet and sullen. Her mood didn't go unnoticed. Mrs Gains seemed to take great pleasure in seeing her in such a way and delighted in the girl's misery.

'Ay-up, missy,' she said as she washed the vegetables. 'Aye, you, with the face that's looks like it sucked a lemon.'

Lizzy gave her a sneer. It wasn't something she was brought up to do.

'Looks like you've lost a shilling and found a penny.' Mrs Gains laughed.

'Who's lost a shilling?' Mr Gains came into the kitchen.

'Toffee nose over there. Not like home, is it, missy? No one here to fetch and carry for you.'

'Probably homesick, Ede.' Mr Gains's sarcasm made his wife grin.

'Homesick for their maid more than likely. I reckon her mum couldn't wait to get rid of her—bloomin' moping around the house like that.'

Charlie and May sat uneasily and picked at their breakfast while Lizzy got annoyed.

'Aye, that face could curdle milk,' Mr Gains laughed.

'They comes up here and think they owns the house? Tells me what I can and can't lose. I tell you, miss nose, the old lady's broke. Dead broke. There ain't no cash for you when she goes.'

'What do you mean?' Lizzy said.

'What she said, missy,' Mr Gains said. 'If you and your mum's looking for a handout, she ain't got nothin left. Spent it all, she has.'

'We don't need money, we don't know her, and we didn't ask to come here,' Lizzy said.

'Don't know her? Didn't ask to come here?' There was a sneer of disbelief on Mrs Gain's face. 'It's not how it works, missy. People don't choose where they're evacuated. You go where you're sent. You're here at her bidding, which makes me wonder why.'

'Maybes she not as broke as she makes out,' her husband said, and he curled his lips.

'So, how come you know her, then?' Mrs Gains frowned at Lizzy being the eldest.

'We don't know her.'

'Don't know her? So, why did she talk about you for these past two months if you don't know her? Answer me that, missy.'

'I don't know anything about her talking about us?'

'Aye, Lizzy this and Charlie that, and Munch when they arrive. Went on all hours,' Mr Gains said.

'That's all she's gone on about for these past months rotten. Lizzy, Charlie and Munch,' his wife said.

'She hardly talked about anything else. We have to get things ready for you when you come, she says. Do this, do that. All about keeping some promise she made.' Mr Gains sounded angry.

Lizzy insisted. 'But we don't know her.'

'Well, she knows you, and that's for sure.' Mrs Gain's head snapped around like an irritated hen. 'Oi, what's that? Where did you get that? That belongs to the missus, don't it?' she barked. She was looking at the prancing hare brooch pinned to May's jumper. 'You been stealing, have you? I knew yous lot were no good.'

May jumped in fear.

'No. Miss Inglestone gave it to May.' Lizzy said.

'Gave it to her? She gives people she don't know expensive gifts, is that what you're saying?' Mr Gains said.

'She did give it to her,' Lizzy stuttered.

'I've fetched and carried for that old biddy for last five year. She owes me more'n wages for cleaning up after her.' Mrs gains looked as though she might rip the brooch of May's jumper.

Lizzy shuddered, and Mrs Gains glared at them.

'I'm telling the truth, Mrs Gains. We don't know how she knows us.'

'She asked for you 'specially, missy,' Mrs Gains said, 'and no one does that.'

'You lot are here because you knows her,' Bill Gains said, 'and she knows you. And, if you think you toffee nose lot are going to steal what's ours, you can think again.'

'We're not toffee noses, were not. And we don't steal.' Charlie shouted.

'What did you say to Bill?' Mrs Gains leered across the table at Charlie.

'Are you deaf? I said we're not toffee-nosed.'

'Don't you talk to me like that? You little brat.'

She lunged towards Charlie, and Lizzy jumped up to stand between them.

'Leave him alone.'

'Get out of my way, missy or I'll give you some as well.' Mrs Gains raised her hand.

Lizzy stood her ground, and Mrs Gains stopped, unsure of herself.

'Apologise, you little brat! You apologise!'

'No, I won't.'

'You little monster.'

'I'll tell Miss Inglestone,' Lizzy threatened.

'Tell her what you bloomin' want. Then who'd clean up and cook for her? You?'

They glared at each other. Lizzy refused to move even though her legs quivered. Mrs Gains's eyes burned with anger. Her face darkened. She balled her fists, and she shook with rage.

'Okay. Enough. Ede, stop, or they'll go running to 'er, an we'll be out on our ear.' Mr Gains grasped his wife's wrist and pulled her away. She swore under her breath and went to the sink, shaking with anger.

'You better watch your mouth.' Mr Gains pointed to Charlie. 'Or I swear, you'll all get the back of me hand, friends of her or not.'

The kitchen was an ugly place, and it frightened Lizzy.

Her legs were shaking, and she had to lean on the table to steady herself. Charlie had a moment to ponder his rebellion, and he trembled so much that May took his hand.

Mrs Gains turned on her heels, a fire raging inside her, and she went outside. Her husband followed. Fearful of what they would do, Lizzy went to the door to see what was happening.

'You should have let me thump her,' Mrs Gains growled. 'You saw that brooch?'

'I did. It's the biddy's all right.'

'Aye, it is. An' I bet there's more from where that came from.'

'There's plenty more over there,' Mr Gains looked towards the ruined manor. 'That boy knows about it. He'll tell me when I find him, by God, he will. Until then, you mind your temper. For now, we have to keep the old hag sweet.'

'Oh, sweet as pie, husband.'

'I'm going to the village.' He smiled and gave her a wink.

The darkness vanished from his wife's face until she saw Lizzy watching, and she scowled.

'Maybe you can buy me that bonnet I want, Billy.'

'Aye,' he said, laughing as he walked away. 'I got some cash.' He drew out a five-pound note from his pants pocket. 'That red one, ain't it?'

'Heard enough, have you, miss nose?' Mrs Gains laughed.

# Chapter 18

For the next few days, an uneasy truce was in force. Lizzy made sure they kept their distance from the Gains. Few words were exchanged, and nothing was said about the incident in the kitchen. As she lay in bed at night, Lizzy heard Mr Gains. He was making a racket, drunk and loud, shouting and cursing. Once, she heard a crash, and Mrs Gains hushed him with loud whispers. He was surly and wolfed his breakfast the following morning before leaving the lodge. By contrast, Mrs Gains was cheerful. She had a new bonnet, a fashionable red pillbox hat with a veil and a feather hair clip. She took great care to put it on in front of the children before she left to go shopping.

The Allens went to Miss Inglestone's room every night before bedtime. It was a pleasant time, something they enjoyed and looked forward to. Miss Inglestone was full of stories about her time in South America. Her eyes sparkled as she took them away to mysterious and exotic places.

Though Lizzy had not mentioned the argument in the kitchen, she suspected that Miss Inglestone knew. But neither said anything. Lizzy asked Mrs Inglestone how she knew of them several times. The old lady was evasive. She never gave a straight answer and mumbled incoherently. She always brought the topic back to their day, how it went, what they saw and did, and their plans for the next one.

May was always first to greet the old lady in the mornings. After breakfast, they wandered the open fields and the village. Staying in the lodge meant being confined to their room or coming under the watchful gaze of Mrs Gains and her barbed tongue.

Even though it was cold, it was a relief to be outside.

The December weather was changeable. Some days dawned cloudy and grey, but there was a freshness different from smoggy London in the air. Other days were glorious, with blue skies and bright sunlight that hurt the eyes. It made the shadows intense black, and the frost sparkled like diamonds.

When they didn't go to the village, they wandered the grounds of the broken-down manor. They stood by the two lonely pillars on either side of the gravel path, from where they could see the entrance to the hall. It felt as if the manor was drawing them nearer, exerting a magnetic attraction, and pulling them closer each day.

Lizzy had written to her mother, as promised. She focused on the good things and didn't mention anything that would worry her. The train journey was long, she wrote in the first. Susan's biscuits were delicious. War and Peace was progressing. She tried to keep it cheerful and wrote about old Miss Inglestone and how pleasant she was and the stories she told. The Gains were mentioned in passing, but only to say that nobody liked them. She didn't write about the loss of the five-pound note and was ashamed and embarrassed, as she was the one trusted with its safekeeping. Charlie and May always added postscripts that Lizzy read before sending—she didn't want anything upsetting their mother. She asked about Susan and added how much they missed her cooking, which was to say, how much they missed her.

On the way to post their latest letter, they walked past the asylum. Holcombe House was an old Victorian workhouse surrounded by a high wall topped with broken glass. An imposing red brick building, it stood on a rise. Iron bars guarded the windows. A pale face, gaunt and skeletal, looked at them from one of the higher windows. Lizzy saw his hands clutching the bars, and a shiver ran up her spine.

'It looks grim. It's like a prison.'

'To keep the loonies in. That's what the lady said.' Charlie said, seeing the face.

'She also said they torture them,' Lizzy reminded him, and Charlie looked away.

The two young prisoners of war they had seen harangued by the boys were by the gates. They were only boys themselves and were busy repairing the hinges. They waved, said something, and then broke out in a hearty laugh.

It was an odd sight, seeing them, the enemy as if they were free and living among them. Lizzy looked, but there were no guards around. She was worried. However, she knew they hadn't escaped, not if they stood plainly for everybody to see. One of them removed his cap and bowed. 'I hope you are well. We are well, also very much.'

Lizzy said they were well, and May and Charlie giggled.

'We are liking very much it here. It is a nice day?'

'It is very pleasant, indeed.'

'I think it will schnee. Schnee?' He made a fluttering

sign with his finger seeing that they didn't understand. He turned to his friend and shouted, 'Karl, was ist schnee?'

'Snow,' his friend shouted back.

'Yes, yes. I think it will snou, also.'

Lizzy said she thought so as well.

'My name is Dieter, and he is Karl.' Karl waved as Lizzy told him their names.

'Gut-day, mein freund. It was gut to speak.' He bowed and walked back to his friend.

The Allens walked on. May and Charlie giggled, but a severe look from Lizzy made them quiet. A second later, they were all giggling. When May glanced back and waved, one of the boys returned it with a sweeping theatrical bow.

After they posted the letter, they went to the library to return the book and saw Milly. She had her customary supply of biscuits and was happy to share them, just as May was happy to eat them. When she saw May's prancing hare, she commented how pretty it was. 'Eh, it proper suits you, lass,' and they chatted like old friends. But the talk was mainly about treasure.

They said goodbye and walked back. Charlie and May pestered Lizzy about visiting the manor. Lizzy nodded but didn't answer them. Her thoughts were reawakened with the library visit. Ted said Mr Gains had money to spend in the pub. And now Mrs Gains had a new hat. Unwelcome thoughts about the missing five pounds crept into her mind.

# Chapter 19

That night, snow fell. Fat flakes drifted from a lowering grey sky. The wind picked up and howled a gale until dawn, with a blast so cold it stung the flesh. Like Milly said, it moaned like lost voices crying in the dead of night from the darkness. By morning, the wind had died, and the moors wore a white blanket as far as the eyes could see. An eerie silence hung across the pristine moorland.

From the bedroom window, Charlie gazed at the miraculous transformation.

'The German boy said it would *schnee,*' he said happily.

At the first sign of snow in London, they'd be up Hampstead Heath and sliding down Parliament Hill on makeshift sledges. But this was different from the neatly enclosed fields of the Heath. The moors stretched to infinity below a transparent blue sky. It was wild and lonely and seemed devoid of life, and a magical, beautiful place in the snow. And there was a great urge to get out into it.

Lizzy told Mrs Gains that they'd be spending time outside and asked if they could have sandwiches. Mrs

Gains pointed to the breadboard and went about her chores.

Before they left, the children visited Miss Inglestone. She was sitting in an armchair by the French window and was wrapped up even though the bedroom was warm. She looked out through the drawn net curtains towards her beloved manor that the snow made exotic. She was lost in thought. When she realised they were there, she gave them a welcoming smile and said how beautiful the manor looked in the snow.

'I wish I was your age—just for a moment, a single tiny moment to play out there again,' Miss Inglestone laughed.

Lizzy thought it was the manor Miss Inglestone longed to play in, not the snow. And when she said to take care, Lizzy understood. Miss Inglestone knew where they were going. She expected her to discourage them, like Ted, the policeman had. Instead, she got the impression that Miss Inglestone wanted them to go there.

'Today will be a special day.' There was happy anticipation in her voice as she spoke to May.

Dressed against the icy cold, they walked as fast as conditions underfoot allowed. Their feet crunched into the snow and it squeaked as they trudged to the manor. The air was sparkling clean. With every breath, they exhaled a puff of white mist. When they reached the pillars between the snow-covered gravel path, they saw their footsteps tracing a long curve back to the lodge. The deep shadows of their footfall picked out in the brilliant sunlight. Ahead of them lay the wreck of Inglestone Manor.

'We must keep together and be careful where we tread.' Lizzy cautioned them when she saw the excited look on May's face.

'This is going to be brilliant,' May gushed.

There were two magnificent oak doors at the entrance protected under a colonnade. They were intricately carved and sculpted. Above the door, chiselled into the stone, a capital letter I was surrounded by laurel leaves. Once the entrance would have shone with wax and varnish, but time and neglect had faded it to a dull grey. The doors were ajar, but swollen with damp, stuck, and the children had to squeeze through.

They were in an expansive foyer with a long corridor. The detritus of over twenty years of abandonment and wanton vandalism lay around them. The ceiling was broken, and light streamed down through holes from the upstairs. Great shafts of solid light in the semi-darkness illuminated the floor like spotlights in a theatre. Snow had fallen through the gaps and lay patched on the once beautiful parquet floors, a testament to the shattered roof. In places, the internal walls had collapsed and lay in piles of rubble.

The children trod carefully and entered a great room. The wallpaper had peeled and hung in ribbons, touching the floors. The snow outside lay in drifts adding additional light to the scene from the broken windows. One of the chandeliers was held precariously from the ceiling by its cord. The other two were fallen and smashed. The twisted metal looked like the skeletons of mythical creatures slain on the floor in the large room. The gutted remnants of sofas and chairs seemed as dead as the imaginary gorgons. Their springs protruded from long slashes, with their stuffing innards hanging out. A grand piano leaned on one surviving leg, its intestine of wire and steel spiralled from the strutted lid in a wild tangle.

'This must be the ballroom,' Lizzy said.

She imagined the room vibrant with conversation,

heard the music, and felt the joy that must have existed here. In her mind's eye, she saw Miss Inglestone, young and spirited, swirling to a waltz in the arms of her *amante*. It made her happy and sad at the same time, but the ghosts of the past were not hers to disturb.

They returned to the corridor and stood at the base of a grand staircase. It was the one Mrs Inglestone descended to have her photograph taken. The steps swept up to a landing and divided into two, rising in an elegant curve to balconies overlooking the ground floor. In the semi-darkness, they noticed more rooms along the corridors above them. Lizzy marvelled at the magnificence the fire catastrophe had ended. It left only a shadow in its wake.

Somebody had taken a hammer and crowbar to the walls. Each room they entered had the same damage. Where the panelling would have been, huge gashes rendered the house's bones and exposed them. The floorboards had been pulled up in places, exposing the joists and beams.

Charlie wanted to go upstairs, but Lizzy said they should explore the ground floor first. They avoided the stairs leading down to the kitchen; the stone steps disappeared into a cold and black void that felt inhospitable.

In the quiet house, any sound was magnified; the creaking floorboards seemed louder, and their footsteps echoed, disappearing ahead of them down empty corridors.

May stood apart and shouted, 'Is anyone home?' She laughed as he heard the echoes bouncing around her.

'Is there anyone here?' Charlie shouted.

'Whoo, just me. I am the ghost of Inglestone Manor, and I have come back for the treasure,' May shouted in a deep voice. She ran a circle around Lizzy and Charlie, with her arms in front of her.

Above them, they heard the flapping of wings. Birds, disturbed by the noise, struggled to get away. They crashed and scraped in a clatter, rising to a crescendo before dying away as they found a hole in the roof to their freedom. The ruins fell silent.

They'd explored all the rooms on the ground floor by lunchtime, except for the kitchen with the entrance to the cellar below and the dangerous fire-gutted wing. So they only peeked inside. They saw fallen smoke-blackened beams and the powder blue sky above; the floor was thick with snow. They returned to the ballroom and sat on the floor between old, gutted sofas. Lizzy gave them a sandwich each.

'This must have been a beautiful place,' Lizzy said.

'To think Miss Inglestone grew up here,' Charlie said.

'It must be frustrating to live so close and know that the place is a ruin when she could remember what it used to be like.'

'I would be sad.'

'It could get fixed up,' May said. She looked around optimistically.

'It would cost a fortune,' Lizzy said.

'If we find the treasure, we could give it to Miss Inglestone, and she could get it done.'

'Where would we look? And anyway, she's so old I think it would be too much for her to consider it.'

'Do you think the treasure hunters did the damage?' Charlie asked.

'Some of it, I guess,' Lizzy said. 'What a mess they've made. With all the fire and water damage, no one will find the diamonds if Mr Inglestone hid them here. The house has been empty since 1919—that's a long time, and it does look as if someone's had a good search for them.'

'The policeman said the village boys play here. They must have made a lot of mess as well.'

'This is a brilliant place to play,' May said.

'Yes, you don't have to worry about breaking anything because it's all broken anyway,' Charlie said.

May got up and found a stick. She wandered about the room, using it to turn things over and move stuff out of the way. She got as far as the broken windows and peered out of each one and all around her.

'This is the best day ever. It's even better than when Mummy took us on Aunt Marie's boat. Or when Daddy took us to that posh hotel, we had scones with jam and cream.'

'And then you were sick all over Susan,' Lizzy reminded her.

'It was still the best jam and cream ever.' Suddenly she stopped. 'Lizzy?' she whispered.

'What is it, Munch?'

'Lizzy, come here,' she whispered insistently.

'What is it?'

There were footprints in the snow that had driven in through the broken windows and roof. They were small—from a little person, and curiously, they led out of the house. Someone had been in here with them and had left the building via the ballroom. When she looked outside, the prints went along the perimeter, disappearing around the corner of the building.

They followed the tracks to where they entered the building through another window.

'Do you think it's the boy Mr Gains been looking for?' Charlie asked.

'Maybe it was one of the village boys playing here,' Lizzy said.

'Hello. Is anyone here?' May shouted.

They waited, but there was no reply. She shouted again, and nobody answered. Whoever was here, they had either snuck out, or they didn't want to be found.

By mid-afternoon, the sun was dipping, and the cold bit through their clothing, so they left Inglestone Manor.

The path they made in the snow on the way there had been crossed several times. The big boot prints suggested it might be by Mr Gains. The intruder must have come to the manor using a different route.

'We'll search the upstairs tomorrow,' Lizzy said. 'With Christmas so soon, maybe we can find something to give Miss Inglestone. If there's something that hasn't been damaged, it would be a lovely reminder of the place.'

'Christmas.' May said, clearly thinking about home.

'Like what?' Charlie asked to distract her.

'I'm not sure. But there must be something we can give her,' Lizzy said.

When they got back, Mrs Gains was by the stove, and her face had the same surly look from when they left that morning. She barely acknowledged their arrival. May didn't want to be in the kitchen with her and went to see Miss Inglestone to tell her about their adventures.

# Chapter 20

Miss Inglestone sat up in bed. The blankets were drawn around her as she listened to May. She asked a lot of questions: did they see this or that? What did the drawing-room look like?—'Oh, those chandeliers, they were so beautiful.' It saddened her that the place was a ruin, and even though she hadn't seen it for many years, she couldn't bear to think about the manor in such a state. The last time she was there was in its prime, in the 1890s.

'That was when I brought my Carlos to see father, and not long after that, we sailed away. Father was pleased even though it was unusual for a young woman to travel in those days—but then he was an unusual man. Munch, he knew things and had an uncanny knack for knowing before events happened. So, he knew we would be all right. Alas, that was the last time I saw my father. I did not find out what happened until many years after the fire. And by then, I had my life in Buenos Aires. There was nothing left for me to return to.'

'Not even the treasure?' May asked.

Miss Inglestone's face brightened, and she laughed. 'Not even the treasure, Munch. There is more to life than pretty trinkets. My father's letter explained everything. He must have written it a month before the fire. He wrote that since I was well provided for, and I was, the jewels did not matter. You see, I could not have children, and he knew that I would be the last of the Inglestones—after me, there was nobody left to inherit. They will never be found, he told me that in his letter. Never! He was adamant. I do not know what he did with them.' She looked at the photograph of him. Something passed across her face that made her smile. 'But I wish I had seen him before he died. I have few regrets, Katherine May Allen. And not seeing my father again is one of them.'

'Our father is fighting in France,' Charlie said. The memory came swiftly to the small boy, and the light left his face. 'I wish he was home.'

'You miss him, don't you, child?'

Charlie didn't answer; he didn't need to.

The fire cracked and threw sparks in the air, and in the darkened room, the flamelight flickered across the walls and lit the kind faces looking down on them.

Lizzy looked at Charlie, and they smiled sadly at each other.

'We saw some footprints,' May said.

'Footprints, Munch?'

'There was someone there,' May whispered.

Miss Inglestone leaned her head to one side in a question.

'She means we saw some footprints that weren't ours. They were in the snow, so it must have been recent,' Lizzy said.

Miss Inglestone said, 'Mr Gains perhaps?'

'No. It was from small feet, like ours.'

'One of the boys from the village, then?'

'It could be. But we didn't see anyone.'

'And you plan to go there again?'

'Yes,' May said excitedly. 'Tomorrow, we're going to explore the top floor.'

'Munch.' Lizzy said. She glared a warning at May to hold her tongue, but the small girl had a huge smile.

'But Lizzy, we have to. And it's not a secret from Miss Inglestone.'

'You must be careful,' Miss Inglestone said, 'I suspect it is more dilapidated than below.'

Lizzy nodded.

'Ah, The bedrooms. There's a playroom up there as

well, and a nursery. Do you know, May, my father was an explorer?' The girl's eyes widened. 'When he was your age, he would disappear for days. The manor was such a big place to explore. He would never tell anyone where he went—remembering what nanny told us.'

May leaned in for a secret. 'What did nanny tell you?'

Lizzy grinned, and to spare the old lady, she whispered. 'Ask me no questions, and you'll be told no lies.'

Miss Inglestone laughed.

'When I was very young, Munch, Father used to tell me about his adventures. I was fascinated. He had such an imagination. Will you tell me about yours?'

May grinned.

As they were leaving, Miss Inglestone asked Lizzy to stay. She wondered if they were happy at the lodge and, not wanting to upset her, Lizzy said, yes. Her mother once told her it's rude for guests to complain, and she didn't want to tell her how unhappy the Gains made them.

'Do you believe in fate?' Miss Inglestone asked.

Lizzy didn't know how to answer the question.

'I do, though I do not pretend to understand it. I have

been given a rare gift, Elizabeth, and a chance to make a lost dream real. It has been a burden, bringing me back here after all those years away. But it's one I am happy to undertake. There will be a measure of justice through it, but I don't understand that either. All I know in my heart is everything will come right. I hope I am up to the task. I feel as if I have been waiting to do this all my life. Things are destined for so many strange reasons.'

Miss Inglestone seemed as old as she was and as vulnerable and fragile. Lizzy wanted to ask her what the gift was? What will be put right? And waiting for what? But Miss Inglestone smiled and changed the subject. The moment was gone.

# Chapter 21

For the rest of the week, the children went to the manor every day. They explored the first floor with great care. For over twenty years, inclement weather had invaded the mansion through its broken roof and shattered windows and wrecked the floors. They trod carefully, testing the strength of the boards with small steps to be sure that they were safe to walk across.

The size of the upstairs rooms hinted at the magnificence of the manor and indicated its former grandeur. In places, the roof had collapsed, bringing down some of the vast attics. The weight of the debris caused the floor to sag and give way, and there were holes where they could see the rooms below. Swathes of the sky with scudding clouds could be seen through the broken ceilings.

But the search for Miss Inglestone's Christmas present was futile. Years of looting, vandalism, and abandonment had left nothing of value. They had no idea what they hoped to find, and Lizzy said they'd know when they found it. May brought several things over for scrutiny. Recognising them for what they were, Lizzy shook her

head.

They found the same destruction in the nursery as everywhere else. What was left of a crib was smashed. The wooden bars had all been snapped. The toys they'd expected to be there were long gone. Cupboards had doors ripped off their hinges, and the shelves were dusty and bare. The room looked sad.

'All the Inglestones grew up in this room,' Lizzy said. 'They'd have had nannies looking after them. There were probably loads of toys and things to play with. When I close my eyes, I can imagine what it must have been like.'

Charlie and May closed their eyes, listening for the sound of the laughter from the playing children.

'Do you think they had someone like Susan?' May asked.

Lizzy nodded. 'Twenty Susans, I imagine. They would have stood right here.' Lizzy walked to the window and felt the shadow of the former employees touch her.

The surrounding countryside spread all around her. The lodge and trees surrounding it were a dark smudge in the snow, and beyond that, she could see the village's roofs. Holcombe House was an imposing solid block of red bricks at the edge of the town. The river, reflecting the sky, glinted like silver blue steel and the railway line, against a dark embankment, cut across the snowy land. It vanished behind the buildings, reappearing on the other side. In the bright sky, birds climbed into the frosty air. It was easy to imagine the manor as a lonely island in the sea of white.

From her vantage point, Lizzy saw tracks in the snow. The ones they'd made were wide and worn and had been traversed many times. Cutting across them were prints that Mr Gains and his dog had made and, in places, she saw some left by small animals. She imagined foxes and hares' neatly spaced steps that meandered towards the hedges.

She saw Mr Gains in the field, with his legs apart and his shotgun across the crook of his arm. He was the only dark object in the white farmland. It was a distance, but it seemed to her that he had a cross look on his face. He straightened his shotgun, and, in a swift, practised motion, he brought the butt up to his shoulder. He fired one barrel. The sharp report made Charlie and May rush to the window. They watched as he broke the gun, and a smoking cartridge flew out. He trudged to a red mass against the white of the snow and lifted a rabbit by its hind legs. Lizzy saw him smile, or so she thought. He turned away and walked back towards the lodge with his kill—stew for supper again.

Afterwards, they continued their exploration of the manor in silence. The image of Mr Gains and the rabbit was heavy in their minds. They saw the footprints, but they didn't lead anywhere in particular as before.

Sometimes they thought they heard footsteps, but their imaginations were heightened, and any sound was more than it was, especially in the deathly quiet of the manor.

'I'm sure someone's looking at us,' May said.

She would turn with a jump, her arms outstretched as if to catch someone before they had a chance to hide. May listened to the noise of the house, and the wind blowing through the holes in the roofs sounding like whispers. Once, she thought she saw a shadow move, and later, she heard a scrambling sound. When she mentioned it, Charlie's eyes rolled to the ceiling.

Lizzy had to admit that their search for a present for Miss Inglestone was fruitless. There was nothing suitable. The vast house was a desert.

'You would think there'd be something.'

'Not a sausage,' Charlie said.

'Well, we have to give her something for Christmas. She's been so kind.' Lizzy said.

'Do we have to get the Gains one as well?' Charlie asked.

Lizzy wanted to get them something, to bury the hatchet, but then remembered how Mrs Gains went for Charlie and said, 'No. Just for Miss Inglestone.'

'We can see what's in the village.'

'That's all we can do, Charlie.'

As they left, there was a loud crash from the adjacent room. The sound was a long creak that turned into a clattering series of bangs. They heard more creaking and snapping above. Part of the ceiling had collapsed. It lay in a heap on the floor, with a mixture of plaster dust and grime creating the illusion of a smoke-screen. The plaster lay among rotting floorboards and dirty snow.

'The weight of the snow brought it down,' Lizzy said.

'The policeman said it was dangerous. We could have been standing there,' Charlie shouted.

They ran as more of the ceiling tumbled down in a cloud of smoky grey dust.

'I saw someone! I did. Really I did! I saw someone,'

May shouted as they left the house. 'On the floor above us. I saw someone looking through the hole.'

'Oh, May, you've been saying that all day,' Lizzy said.

'No, I did!'

'Aye,' Charlie said, imitating Mrs Gains, 'And there's many as wouldn't believe you.' He laughed while Lizzy stifled her mirth at Charlie's impersonation, all to May's annoyance.

As the noise from the avalanche died down, they stood outside in the snow, panting. Their hearts were thumping, wild with excitement. They weren't going back to see the destruction, and as it was still early, they would go to the village.

'I did see somebody, and you two are just mean.' May protested as they trudged along. 'Someone was there, and I bet he's watching us walk away now. He was waiting for his chance to ambush us and capture us at the manor. And he probably fell through the ceiling and is buried under all of that stuff. He might be injured and waiting for us to help him. And we didn't, and he'll probably die before anyone finds him, and then they'll only find his bones. And he would have written in the dust, "*the Allens*

131

*did it*." And then we'd all get arrested and go to jail, and Daddy will have to come…'

'That's a lot of *and's* May,' Lizzy said.

When she realised no one was really paying attention, May sighed and mumbled, 'No one ever believes me.' She kicked the snow with her wellington boots.

'Why would anyone want to capture us?' Charlie said. 'Maybe it was the ghost of Inglestone Manor come to claim another victim—and he's chosen, you, Munch.'

'Oh, haha, Charlie Allen, you think you're so funny.'

Charlie laughed and made ghost noises.

'Shut up.' May shouted.

He ran around May with his arms raised, impersonating a ghost.

'Lizzy, make him stop.'

Lizzy was about to tell Charlie off for teasing when May shouted, 'Look!' and pointed back to the manor.

Lizzy's mouth dropped open. She couldn't make it out with the light behind the estate, but there was no mistaking that somebody was there and watching them. A small, thin figure stared at them from one of the upstairs windows.

'See? I told you.' May said.

'Someone's in there,' Charlie stated the obvious.

'Let's go and find him,' May shouted, and started walking back towards the manor.

A loud boom stopped her as more of the building crashed down. They turned and ran, their hearts thumping with fright and excitement. When they looked again, the figure was gone.

# Chapter 22

'We saw him,' May shouted as she ran into Miss Inglestone's room ahead of Mrs Gains. She was breathless, having run the last hundred yards ahead of everyone else, and her face was a picture of excitement as she jumped on the bed.

'Calm down, child. Who did you see?' Miss Inglestone asked, laughing with the little girl.

'Someone. The ghost. A boy. In the manor. He was spying on us, and I think he almost fell through the ceiling because of this awful crash. We'd run out because we were frightened, and when we looked back, we saw him.'

'A ghost? Who do you think it was?'

'I don't know. We were too scared to go back and look.'

'Your pills, ma'am,' Mrs Gain's face was as black as thunder.

'Thank you, Ede. That's so exciting, May, isn't it?'

'No one believed me when I said I saw someone looking at us. Charlie didn't, and Lizzy didn't. No one ever believes me.'

'Well, I do, May, so tell me all about it.' She patted the bed for the child to sit. 'Get your breath back and start from the beginning.'

Mrs Gains looked over her shoulder when she left the room and scowled at them. May recounted the day's events with enthusiastic gestures.

Mrs Gains was in the kitchen preparing a tray for Miss Inglestone when Lizzy and Charlie came in. She asked Lizzy to wait to carry the tray through. When Charlie left, she said, 'So, you saw the boy, did you?'

'We saw someone,' Lizzy said.

'It were probably him.' Mrs Gains nodded and dismissed Lizzy by ignoring her. She turned to the sink talking, and Lizzy assumed it was to herself. Her voice was more vacant than usual. 'He's a small lad, no more than twelve-year-old. Dressed strangely. So, you know he's escaped from the asylum, don't you? One of them's missing, Ted says. It's not the first time, either. He's always hanging about the manor. He likes hiding there.'

'We were too far away to see him clearly.'

'What was he doing?'

'I don't know. Following us, I think. Who is he?'

'What I said—one of the loonies from Holcombe

House. One gets out and causes a devil of a commotion,' Mrs Gains said. There was a hint of disgust in her voice that she didn't hide.

Lizzy remembered Milly saying something similar— but unlike Mrs Gains, was saddened, especially by what went on inside.

Lizzy reasoned that now that they were alone and Mrs Gains wasn't in a foul mood, they might bury any hatchets.

'I'm sorry if May keeps going on about treasure. She's only little and gets carried away with things.'

Lizzy watched as the woman stiffened, but she carried on when Mrs Gains didn't say anything. 'Maybe there was some once, but the place is a mess. It's been looted for years—and there's nothing left, not so much as an old teapot. I don't think it was ever there to start with if no one's found it after all these years.'

Mrs Gains dried her hands on her apron, contemplating Lizzy. It was as if she had something on her mind. She pulled a chain from under the collar of her dress.

'No, they're there. The diamonds exist all right.'

A small gold ring with a bright red stone dangled from

the chain. She held it up, and the gem glinted in the light.

'This is one Billy found. Took it fair an' square he did, finders keepers. So—the treasure's there all right.'

'Doesn't the ring belong to Miss Inglestone?'

'Belongs to whoever finds it, missy,' Mrs Gains said, the gruffness returning to her voice. 'Finders keepers. The old sod hid it, couldn't even give it to his daughter, so it was anybody's—and now it's mine.' She was her old self again, and Lizzy sighed. 'The boy's dangerous,' Mrs Gains continued. 'He's a mean one, and he'll do you harm. Let me know if you see him again. Billy will deal with him.'

Lizzy could only imagine how Mr Gains would deal with him whatever the boy was and whatever he'd done.

When Lizzy left the kitchen, she felt a connection between the boy and the diamonds. She couldn't say what it was—but she felt it. There was no other reason why the Gains would want him so much. She wondered if she should tell Miss Inglestone about the ring. But what good would that do? It could only make the Gains more unbearable. She decided to keep quiet for now, especially when she heard the joyful noises coming from the old woman's bedroom.

She listened at the door for a while, not wanting to intrude on their fun. But she was troubled. There were too many puzzles and things out of place, like Miss Inglestone's strange conversation about believing in fate. If the Gains were right, how did Miss Inglestone know about their arrival months before being sent to the lodge? Miss Inglestone asked for them especially—that was unusual. She was sure her mother didn't know the Inglestones. They'd never been mentioned at home, and her mother's decision to send them away was a recent one. It wasn't even on the horizon months ago. But the Gains's said Miss Inglestone spoke about them—and knew them by name. Another mystery concerned the missing money and what the policeman told them about Mr Gains having money to spend in the pub. And now there was the boy from the asylum. There were a lot of questions—but no answers.

# Chapter 23

The next day Lizzy's mind was still troubled. She couldn't sort through her thoughts, and the night had been restless. As they walked to the manor, she was quiet. She managed a smile and chatted half-heartedly to her brother and sister, but her mind was elsewhere.

'I bet the treasure's in the nursery. That's where I'd put it.' May said.

'You're only thinking of toys. This is a grown-up treasure. It's got to be somewhere where no one would look. Otherwise, they'd have found it by now. It'll be in the master bedroom locked in a safe.' Charlie said.

'In a safe? There are barely any walls to hide a safe behind, and it's meant to be hidden, remember?' Lizzy laughed at their wild theories.

'The kitchen? Or the cellar?' May said.

'Somewhere else. Everyone's looked there already,' Charlie said.

'Well, where then?'

'Maybe he hid it outside in the grounds.'

'You mean buried it?' May asked.

'That's what I'd do.'

'Then there's bound to be a treasure map. There's always a map.'

'You're right, Munch. There must be one. Take thirty-three paces north from the old Oak, turn ninety degrees left, and walk ten steps to the well.' Charlie walked as if he was pacing out a distance.

'Is there a well?' May asked.

'I'm just making it up. There's always a well. And you have to look under a large rock,' Charlie said.

'Where's the map? He'd have to hide that, as well.'

'Somewhere where nobody would look, of course.'

'I would hide it in the library,' May said with a decisive nod.

'Why there?'

'Because there'd be lots of books there, and no one would expect a map to be in one of them—like where Lizzy hid the money.'

'Yes, they would. They'd look in all of them. It would be one of the first places they'd think of.'

'Then where would he hide it, Mr Clever clogs?'

'Not someplace obvious like that…'

'Will you two shut up about treasure,' Lizzie barked. 'There's is no such thing, not in this mansion anyway.

And if there is, it's gone forever. Now be quiet.'

Lizzy's outburst shocked them. An icy hush descended, broken only by the crunch of their feet in the snow and the wind rustling the bushes.

Lizzy regretted her tone. She could hear her mother's voice saying there would be times when Charlie and May would be difficult and how she had to be patient because she was the eldest. Her heart sank and her head drooped. She felt the heaviness in the air and whispered, 'Sorry, May. Sorry, Charlie. I didn't mean to shout. It's just that a lot has happened, and I wish mum was here.'

They held hands and all had the same wish.

'Maybe there is a treasure map. I mean, it makes sense. That's what I would have done as well, Charlie.'

'Yes,' May cried. 'There's a treasure map.'

'There might be,' Lizzy reminded her.

'But where do we look?' Charlie said.

They gazed at the monstrous edifice, knowing it could be anywhere—if it existed at all.

'Well, we're not going to look today. I've had enough talk about treasure and the like. Anyway, we've still to get Miss Inglestone's present.'

May watched as a plane in the far distance turned and

rolled. Its thrumming engine was a monotonous drone as it headed towards them. It rose steeply, and at the top of its climb, it seemed to just fall away, rolling over, spinning and plummeting to the ground. Its engine was a coughing splutter. It trailed black smoke, and the sun glinted off its wings.

'It's going to crash!' May shouted.

At the last second, the engine spluttered, gunned, and the sound changed to a deep guttural growl as it coughed into life. It climbed in an aerobatic twist and banked before dropping towards the children. It roared overhead at less than a hundred feet in a thunderous boom, and the backwash blew the loose snow around them.

May and Charlie screamed in joy as the aircraft banked.

'It's a Spitfire,' Charlie shouted over the engine's roar.

'Wave at him. Come on, wave,' May shouted.

They waved as the plane thundered overhead, and the pilot waggled the wings in greeting.

Turning away, the aircraft then swept towards them as it came out of the arc. The sound was so deafening that May and Charlie put their hands over their ears, crouching low and Lizzy clutched her hat. The plane thundered overhead. It was flying closer still and whipped up a snow spray. They were thrilled when the pilot did a whole victory roll as he climbed into the sky.

Soon, the plane did a slow ascent towards a blue gap in the clouds. It levelled out, and the engine's growl fell away as the pilot throttled back. He flew past them at a modest speed. He was low enough for them to see into the cockpit, and he waved. They waved back in delight.

'I'm going to be a pilot,' Charlie said, still waving.

'Hello,' May said.

Lizzy turned and was shocked to see her sister standing near a young boy. He wore a dirty raincoat. The boy looked afraid and glanced around nervously. His face was a picture of amazement. His eyes pointed skywards and watched the vanishing plane. He noticed May first, then Lizzy and Charlie, and backed away from them, moving towards a pile of fallen bricks.

'I'm May.' She held out her hand. It seemed a ludicrous thing to do—but that was May.

He kept backing up, and May walked nearer. He almost stumbled when he reached the bricks and had nowhere else to go.

'What was that?' he stammered, the look of wonder

imprinted on his face and the engine's roar still filling their ears.

'A Spitfire, I think,' May said.

'A spitting fire? Is it a dragon?'

'No, a Spitfire, it's an aeroplane,' Lizzy said.

Perhaps, because they seemed friendly and clearly didn't pose a threat, the boy appeared to have given up on running. There was an awkward look on his face as if he was trying to make sense of what she'd said. He mouthed the word 'Spitfire?'

'It must be fantastic to be a pilot, don't you think?' Charlie said.

'Who are you?' Lizzy asked. She didn't move in case she frightened the boy. The trapped look was back, and she could see he wanted to run but was frozen in his confusion. 'Are you the one following us?'

He didn't say anything.

'Did you hurt yourself yesterday when the ceiling caved in?' May asked.

'We're the Allens, and we live over there.' Lizzy pointed to the lodge. 'I'm Lizzy, that's May, and this is Charlie.'

'My name is Abel.'

A dog barking jolted him out of his wonder. Before they could stop him, he was running towards the open window of the manor, shouting, 'Run. He's coming.'

'Who's coming?' Lizzy shouted though she suspected she already knew.

The boy was through the window and gone.

Sabre bounded across the snow from around the corner of the building. His muscular body was lean and his sinews rippled. May and Charlie cried out in fear and ran to Lizzy. She pushed them behind her and stood between them and the dog. They were frozen with fear. The Alsatian fixed its sharp brown eyes on them. With saliva dripping from its bared fangs, it growled, circled them, and it pawed the ground as it edged closer. Its head dropped down, and it crouched, ready to leap.

'Down, Sabre, down, I say. Down, you damn dog.'

Puffing and red in the face, Mr Gains ran to them. His shotgun was locked, and he shouted at the dog. Sabre growled and snarled at his master.

'Down, I say.'

Mr Gains kicked the dog, and it whined but didn't stop snarling. However, it came out of the attacking stance and retreated behind its master. The dog sat in the snow, looking at them as if nothing had happened.

May and Charlie burst into tears and clung to Lizzy.

'Where is he?' Mr Gains shouted.

'Where is who?' Lizzy shouted back. Her legs were shaking, and it was all she could do to muster the courage to answer him.

'The boy. I saw him with you. Where's the beggar gone?' Mr Gains's eyes bulged. He looked around with stabbing glances.

'Your dog could have killed us,' Lizzy said.

'The boy. Where is he?'

'What boy? What are you talking about?'

'Don't you give me any of that, missy.' He pointed at Lizzy. 'Sabre wouldn't have run if he weren't here.'

'Does it look like there's another boy here?' Lizzy said.

Mr Gains glared at her. He grasped Lizzy's shoulders, and his beery breath blew into her face.

'Don't you be telling me your lies, missy.' He shook her.

'Leave me alone.'

Mr Gains glanced around, cursing loudly.

'Let my sister go,' Charlie shouted at him.

Mr Gains saw the footprints in the snow leading to the window. Lizzy felt his anger as he clutched her shoulders, and the fury in his eyes blazed. She looked back in defiance. Her mouth closed, waiting for a blow. She was sure he was going to hit her.

Instead, he pushed her away and whistled the dog. Sabre jumped up and trotted behind him as he stomped across the field to the manor.

'You lot get away from here. It's private property. Go on,' he shouted to his dog, 'get him,' and Sabre bounded away.

May and Charlie were crying and clinging to Lizzy. She crouched between them, her legs about to collapse, and pulled them closer.

'Shush, it's over now. He's gone. So is his dog.'

Lizzy kept a tight grip on their hands and felt them shivering. They were terrified as she led them away. They couldn't do anything to help Abel, and Lizzy hoped he'd get away all right. They walked across the frozen fields to the lodge.

# Chapter 24

It was hours before May and Charlie recovered from their fright, and Lizzy just as long, though she put on a braver face. To calm down and escape into another world, they read War and Peace. Lizzy was grateful that Miss Inglestone was already asleep, and they didn't have to visit that night.

They ate supper silently, thankful that Mrs Gains had other things to do and did not remain. After washing the dishes, they crawled upstairs to their bedroom and were soon in bed. In the fretful hours before falling asleep, Lizzy lay awake, remembering the awful look on Mr Gains's face. She was angry and scared, but her mother's words about looking after her brother and sister returned to her. She lay awake, going over what an awful job she was doing.

She thought about Abel. He looked strange and acted weird. But he didn't look mad or as if he belonged in the asylum. She wondered how *do* mad people look. Milly said they look just like you and me? It would be difficult if you couldn't tell if a person was mad when you met them.

She was woken up by whimpering. Her sister had a bad dream that woke her in a cold sweat. Lizzy took May into her bed and wrapped her arms around her. May dipped her head under the blanket. She kept as still as she could and was afraid to move. She was determined to stay awake, and Lizzie knew it was Sabre May saw when she closed her eyes. Lizzie held her close until tiredness overcame May's resistance, and only when her sister slept, did she.

Like her sister, Lizzy fell into uneasy dreams with the barking dog taking a leading role.

*** 

In the morning, May was sullen, and she stayed close to Lizzy in the presence of Mrs Gains.

Mrs Gains took pleasure in calling them toffs and spoilt and revelled in their experience with the dog.

May picked at her food without an appetite. When Charlie tried to cheer her up, she turned away. Before finishing, May asked for permission to leave the table. She went back to the bedroom and slipped under the blankets.

When Mr Gains came in, Lizzy and Charlie finished eating. Mr Gains had overslept and was suffering from a hangover. He was wearing the same clothes as the day before, and they were creased as if he'd slept in them. He dipped his head under the cold tap and dried his face with a kitchen towel that he discarded on the counter. Then he mumbled something about tea. He gave Lizzy and Charlie a sharp glance and muttered something.

Lizzy asked Charlie to go and see how May was. She wanted to be alone with the couple. When he left, Lizzy cleared her throat and took a breath to find her courage.

'You've been nasty and unkind ever since we arrived. We haven't done anything wrong and don't understand why you're like that. We haven't done anything to either of you, yet you're making us miserable.'

'You better watch your mouth, missy,' Mr Gains grumbled.

'Or what? You're going to hit me or something? Set your dog on me? We didn't ask to come here, and we don't know Miss Inglestone, even though you don't believe us. We've never met her, and we don't know how she knows us. And I don't know why you want to make our time here so awful.'

'I told you to watch your mouth.'

'We're not toffs or spoilt. We don't want to be here, and we'd rather be in London with all the bombs than here with you. Our mum sent us away because she loves us, not because she wanted to get rid of us. And our father's in France risking his life…'

'Now you listen to me, you little brat.'

'No, I won't. I'm not going to be bullied by you anymore. I'm not afraid of you… or your dog. You're vile people.'

'Who're you calling vile?' Mrs Gains said.

'Both of you. You make fun of us, scare May and Charlie and make us feel unwelcome and in the way.'

'Is this what you want? You insolent, ungrateful so and so.' Mr Gains stepped forward with a raised hand, and it seemed to irritate him when Lizzy didn't cower.

In a shocking slap, he swung his arm and caught Lizzy's cheek with his open palm. She slipped into her chair in wide-eyed terror, with her face stinging. Mrs Gains grabbed her husband's arm before he could land another blow.

'Is that it? Slapping girls. Is that what you do?' Lizzie shouted.

Mr Gains struggled against his wife's grip.

'Leave it be, Billy. Hold your temper, or there'll be trouble from her nibs.'

'She don't get to talk to me like that. No one talks to me like that. You hear me, not you or that old woman, nor her dad, no one? I've laid men cold for less!'

Lizzy stood up quiet in front of the angry man, inviting him to slap her again. She forced back her tears.

'You want more?' he asked.

'I know you stole my money. And I know you have Miss Inglestone's ring. Don't think I won't tell her.' Her legs were trembling. She gripped the table until her knuckles whitened. 'It stops now. If you bully us anymore, then see what'll happen.'

Mr Gains hesitated, but the rage was still in his eyes. He chewed his lip and pulled his arm free from his wife.

'You keep out of my way, do you hear me?'

'And if I don't, will you slap me again? Is that all you can do—beat up girls? And steal from them?'

Lizzy shuddered, wondering if she had gone too far. She kept her eyes fixed on Mr Gains to stare him down.

The blood rushed to his face, giving Lizzy an acidic stare. He stomped into the yard, slamming the door behind him in his fury.

'You bleeding toffs. You think you own the place, do you? I'm warning you…'

'We don't own anything. And we're not here because we wanted to be here.' Lizzy's courage was up. The brand on her face was the price she'd paid for her bravery. She'd been hit for the first time in her life, and it couldn't get any worse than that.

'I've sweated for that woman for years. She owes me more than just a bleedin' thanks. And if you think you can come along and take our dues away, you're mistaken.'

'I don't care if you've sweated for a million years. She pays you for it and owes you nothing more.' Lizzy started to leave the kitchen. Though her legs wobbled and her heart thumped, she was pleased that she'd stood up to them. Daddy once told her it was the only way to deal with bullies. She looked back. 'And if you don't like it, then you can be the ones to go. We haven't come here to take anything. We're here because we were sent.'

'You get back here and do the washing up?' Mrs Gains said.

'That's your job, isn't it?' she said, curling her lips

into a scowl.

She didn't wait for Mrs Gains's reaction but imagined the look on the woman's face must have been fury and utter contempt.

# Chapter 25

Charlie and May were sitting on their bed, and she sat with them. She was fuming but hid her anger from them. May leaned into her, and she wrapped her arms around the small girl's shoulder. Her eyes were watery and sad as if she was about to burst into tears.

'We heard him shouting at you, and we were scared. Are you all right?' Charlie asked.

'I know, Charlie,' Lizzy said.

Charlie saw the bruise on her cheek, and Lizzy stood up to distract him.

'Come on a brisk walk around the grounds, and we'll be right as rain, then we'll say hello to Miss Inglestone. And no more crying or being sad. Is it a deal?'

Lizzy set a fast pace, angry from her encounter with the Gains, and the adrenalin fuelled her blood. The other two trailed behind her. Charlie shouted for her to slow down, but Lizzy's head was low, and she charged along, puffing hard and walking fast. Behind her, Charlie and May struggled to keep up. They called again, but Lizzy drove on. Her mind was back in the kitchen, arguing with Mr Gains. She could smell his beery breath and still felt the sting of his hand against her cheek—and all that did was make her walk faster.

The walk was a steady march, and soon her mind calmed, and the wobbles left her legs. She stopped being angry. Her face still stung, but she didn't mind that anymore—she had stood up to Mr Gains, and it felt good. But more satisfying was hearing May's voice and her shrill laugh, even when Charlie, pretending to be Sabre, barked at her. May stuck her tongue out and giggled. When she complained about being hungry, Lizzy smiled. When she felt a snowball land on her back, she turned to see them staring around, pretending innocence, and the burden was lifted from her.

They'd done two wide circuits around the lodge, and Lizzy stopped. She was hot and panting. She'd made up her mind about going back to the manor. In her defiant mood, nothing was out of bounds. She hadn't thought through what she'd do if Sabre turned up again, but since they were here and there wasn't a thing they could do about it, they had to make the most of it. The Gains were awful people, but Miss Inglestone was kind, as were Milly and Ted. The thought cheered her up.

When they got back, Charlie and May went to see

Miss Inglestone, and Lizzy went to their bedroom. She caught Mrs Gains leaning over her open bedside drawer. The woman stood up and looked back furtively.

'There's nothing in there,' Lizzy said.

'I don't know what you mean.'

'There's only five pounds left, and I've got that in my pocket, so you can't get it,' she lied.

'Are you calling me a thief?'

Lizzy said nothing. She saw the embarrassment and shame on the woman's red face. The missing money had been stolen. She knew that now and Mrs Gains would deny taking it no matter what was said. If she wanted an argument, Lizzy was happy to give her one.

Mrs Gains slammed the drawer shut with a bang and brushed past Lizzy as she left the room. In her most sarcastic voice, Lizzy shouted, 'Your new hat looks nice.'

Mrs Gains stood with her back to Lizzy as if calming herself. She appeared to take several deep breaths. Her hands opened and closed, making fists. When she walked away, she did so slowly and in control.

'Aye,' she said, over her shoulder. 'It is, in't it? And it were right expensive as well. Maybe you should get one.'

# Chapter 26

When Lizzy went to Miss Inglestone's room, May had regaled her about their encounter with the strange boy. Lizzy detected a change in the old lady's mood. She didn't seem as frivolous and sat with a serious face—half listening. She held her photographic album and thumbed through it. Her eye would shift to a photo and back to the children every now and then.

'How old was he?' she asked. Charlie said about eleven. She nodded and mumbled Charlie's answer back to him, 'Yes, about eleven. And how was he dressed?'

'Funny like.' Charlie screwed his nose as he described what he wore. 'And he acted funny as well.' He couldn't explain what was funny about the way he acted—only that he didn't seem to know much of anything.

He told Miss Inglestone how Sabre had almost attacked them and that it frightened May. The strange boy was frightened, and he ran off as well, he said.

Something dark washed across Miss Inglestone's face, and Lizzy wished Charlie hadn't mentioned it.

Miss Inglestone took May's hand. 'And how is my little soldier feeling now?'

Her question was met with an awkward smile—May was putting on a brave face.

'I think you were very courageous, Munch. Such bravery. I have known many who would have run away and hidden. You are deserving of the gift I gave you. It is your medal.' She brushed a finger across the golden hare.

May gave a smile, and it was mirrored by Miss Inglestone's.

'The Spitfire scared him,' May described the trajectory of the machine with her hand and imitated the sound of the plane as it swooped past.

'I think many things would scare him, Munch. Do you think he is someone that escaped from the asylum? They do escape, and frequently as well, you know.'

'He was acting a bit funny. Following us for days, then hiding and running away,' Charlie said.

Lizzy was to one side of the old lady, aware of Miss Inglestone's eyes scanning her. The bruise on her face had not gone unnoticed. Lizzy suspected she was waiting for an explanation. When she didn't speak, Miss Inglestone did what Lizzy feared most. She asked her directly.

'I am too long in the tooth to be fobbed off with

excuses, Elizabeth, even the excuse of silence. Now, what happened to your face?'

It took Lizzy a few moments, and she spoke with reluctance. She didn't like telling tales out of school, an expression she'd heard Susan using. But Miss Inglestone wouldn't let it go.

Lizzy told her about the Gains's behaviour and how upsetting it was. Once she opened up, it all flooded out. She told her about the missing money and said it had been stolen rather than lost. However, she did not tell her that she thought Mrs Gains was the thief, nor did she mention the ring. At the back of her mind, she wondered if she'd provoked the confrontation in the kitchen by not backing down.

Miss Inglestone moved the hair from Lizzy's face and looked at the red blotch. She asked a lot of questions. Lizzy bowed her head in the quiet that followed, and Charlie and May looked nervously around the room. The silence was oppressive, and Lizzy felt that they should leave to give Miss Inglestone some time to herself. May, broke the silence defiantly.

'We're going back to the manor,' she announced.

Miss Inglestone opened her eyes and nodded, 'Good,'

she closed the photo album with a bang. 'Now, you two. You had better get ready. Go on, off you go. Lizzy, stay awhile.'

Lizzy was worried that she'd got the Gains in trouble. She feared that Miss Inglestone knew about the ring and had figured out who had taken the money. As she rearranged the pillows for her, the old lady said, 'May said that the boy's name is Abel?'

'Yes.'

'Tell me, Elizabeth… does he have scars on his right hand and arm?'

'None that we could see.' It was a curious question, but before Lizzy could ask what she meant, Miss Inglestone moved on.

'Elizabeth, I want you to answer truthfully this time. Are you happy here?'

'Yes,' said Lizzy after a while—she couldn't lie to the old woman. 'I mean, it's different from our home in London, and we miss Mum and Susan, and I miss my friends. But we're ever so grateful, Miss Inglestone. Please don't think we're not, especially with bombs falling around us and Mum being so worried and Daddy away.'

'Grateful?' Miss Inglestone gave a wry laugh. 'There is nothing to be grateful for, child. You've given me so much pleasure being here that it is I that should be grateful.' She lay back against her pillows. A faraway look came to her face. Her eyes gazed at the middle distance and looked at nothing. 'We four miss our fathers, do we not, Lizzy? If I could meet mine again, I would tell him I kept my promise.'

Sadness returned to the old lady. She looked every bit as old and brittle as before. She was silent, then said, 'But now I need to speak to the Gains.'

Lizzy tried to say something to stop her. The feelings of guilt were stronger than ever, and she didn't want to cause trouble. She suspected Miss Inglestone's intentions. But the old lady didn't say any more.

# Chapter 27

Lizzy resisted May's pestering that they should go to the manor because the boy might be there. Her mind was on what Miss Inglestone was going to do. She was worried about the consequences of speaking freely. She decided, instead, they would go to the village.

They walked farther up the stream than before, almost in a circle, before scrambling over the railway embankment and returning to the village near the Red Lion public house. May had found a pebble that she was determined to kick for as long as she could, and she did until she kicked it over a bank, and it disappeared into the bushes.

They went to a chippie in the corner of the main square. The thought of lunch at the lodge depressed Lizzy, and she said it would be nice to eat out.

She ordered three cod and chips, and the lady dished them into newspaper before adding salt and vinegar. They ran to the bridge and sat on a bench by the stream. They could feel the heat from their newspaper-wrapped meal warming their laps and making them ravenous. They waved at a few men on bicycles and a mother pushing a pram. It was that kind of village. Some boys ran past, shouting and having a good time, but they didn't say anything. May threw the odd burnt chip into the ice-cold water of the river, and the ducks made a swift dash to where they landed. They reached out their long dark-green necks and snatched the chips with squawks and splashes. May was delighted.

After lunch, they wandered to the railway station and waited on the empty platform. The stationmaster got fed up with them hanging around and shouted to go away.

'We're waiting for the next train to see who will get off,' Lizzy said.

'Well, young lady, it'll be a long wait—there's nowt due in till morning.' Leaving his office, he chatted with them, and he rubbed his hands together and blew his breath between the closed palms. 'Come on, lass, get off home before it gets too cold. We'll be getting more snow before week's out.'

They said goodbye and went back to the lodge along the frozen path. While Charlie and May had the energy to run, Lizzy was quiet.

It had just gone three when they arrived, and the day was darkening. Mrs Gains greeted them with her customary scowl but made no comments except the Mistress wanted to see Lizzy. Miss Inglestone was where Lizzy had left her that morning, in bed and propped up on pillows.

'I have released the Gains,' Miss Inglestone said plainly. She held up her hand to silence Lizzy. 'They have been given a month's notice and will leave in January. My nurse will arrange a new housekeeper before then.'

Lizzy tried to protest. It was as she feared. As much as she disliked the Gains, she felt their dismissal was her fault.

Miss Inglestone would hear none of it and wouldn't change her mind. She'd done her best to respect her father's wishes, but their behaviour would not be tolerated.

'Father told me he always felt a great responsibility for William Gains, though he never told me why. But father always felt that way about his employees, especially when Billy's father died. I was told to keep him on when I came home. However, I will not countenance such treatment of my guests.'

Before Lizzy told the others, she stood looking

through the open kitchen door at Mrs Gains. She couldn't lose the awful thought that she was responsible for their dismissal. The Allens came to Inglestone in all innocence and were so far from home and afraid in a different world from the one they knew. She wondered what the Gains would do and how trivial the missing money seemed. But her self-pity came to an abrupt end when she remembered Mr Gains's angry face and the slap. The vision of Sabre, barking and snarling, loomed over her and made feeling sorry for them difficult.

When Lizzy told Charlie and May, they were ecstatic. Lizzy admonished them, reminding them that the Gains had lost their jobs which wasn't something to be happy about. Charlie huffed and mumbled, 'Serves them right,' and May, taking the lead from her brother, said the same. Lizzy's stare made them go quiet. Foremost in her mind was the relationship with the angry couple over the following month. She had to look them in their eye, and her guilt was paramount.

That evening supper was a silent affair. The children ate quickly, not wanting to hang around in the kitchen longer than necessary. Mrs Gains kept herself busy and out of the way. She was clearly angry, and the resentment was etched on her face.

As Charlie and May left, Mr Gains came in. He was drunk and swayed, banging into the doorframe. He didn't look at them and hung his shotgun on the hook beside the door. Lizzy wanted to say she was sorry. She felt terrible. But seeing him again at such close quarters, she was frightened of him, and her courage failed. The kitchen felt like an unbearably crowded place. She collected the plates, but Mrs Gains snatched them off her without a word. Her movement was so sudden and unexpected that the pile of dirty dishes almost crashed to the floor.

Before going to her room, Lizzy waited in the hallway, behind the kitchen door.

'I'm going to Leeds tomorrow,' Mr Gains said. 'There's an opening for a gardener and handyman at a big house. I'll ask if they want a cook when I'm there.' Through the gap in the door, she saw him slump into the chair with his head low.

Edith Gains didn't reply.

# Chapter 28

The following day, the children went back to the manor. Charlie and May chased each other, playing in the snow while Lizzy followed. When they entered the old ballroom, they saw the boy.

He was looking at them through one of the holes in the upstairs floor.

While Charlie and May were delighted to see him, Lizzy was angry because he'd run away and left them to the mercy of Sabre. Visions of the snarling dog were still plaguing her mind. The boy didn't look dangerous, as she was led to believe, just queerly funny. If anything, he looked timid and frightened. He didn't indicate being insane, at least not the way she imagined insane people would be, wild-haired and raving.

Before she could say anything, Abel seemed to read her mind, 'Please forgive me. Running away was not a gentlemanly thing to do. I am not a coward, I assure you. I should have stayed, but I was foolish.'

His face was a picture of contrition, his voice pleading, and Lizzy thought his actions worried him, and he'd had time to brood on them. Recalling her own fear and how terrified they were, she couldn't blame him—if the situation were reversed, she might have been just as foolish.

'Why have you been hiding from us?' Lizzy asked.

'I did not know who you were. I thought you might be with the bad man with the gun.'

'That's the groundsman, Mr Gains.'

'He chases me, but he will never catch me. I know where to hide, and I can go places he cannot. I know every inch of the manor, more so than anyone in the world.' He spoke with pride as if he was playing a game.

'Mr Gain has gone away. He won't be back for a few days. You'll be safe until then.'

'We don't like him either,' Charlie said.

'Or his horrible dog,' May added.

The boy edged away until he vanished from view.

'Has he gone?' May asked.

Lizzy nodded. Her first thought was to go after him. If they were quick, they might catch up with him. But he might see it as an attempt to capture him. Perhaps he didn't believe her when she told him about Mr Gains's absence and thought it was a ruse to trap him. There must be others searching for him, like Ted and the people from Holcombe House, so it was understandable that he was doubly frightened and cautious.

She turned to leave when he appeared again. He edged into the room and stood where he could run should he need to. He was nervous, more so now that he was fully exposed. He seemed to be summoning up his courage and must have decided they could be trusted.

'I am the master of Inglestone Manor,' he said. 'It is my pleasure to meet you. Welcome to my house.' He bowed deeply. Then, lifted his head proudly,

'Excuse me?' Lizzy was puzzled.

Charlie giggled, and Lizzy gave her brother a sharp glance. She wasn't worried that the boy was violent if he took offence; her concern was about how small and vulnerable he looked. She felt sorry for him, dressed in his dust-covered clothes. As Milly called them, he was one of the Poor Devils, living in Holcombe House.

'I am afraid there's not much left to be master of. Some people would be scared to be here on their own. We were told that someone burned the manor to cover up a murder,' Lizzy said.

'There have been no murders here. You are mistaken.'

'The lady said there was. Old Mr Inglestone was

murdered by a thief,' Charlie said

It was Abel's turn to laugh, and it took him a second to regain his composure.

'I assure you there have been no murders here. I am sure it is a splendid game you play, but I left my grandfather, healthy and very much alive, after breakfast this morning.' He strutted, with his head high, as if he was indeed master in the wreck of the house.

Charlie's mouth opened in surprise. 'It's not a game. And Miss Inglestone owns the manor, and there has been a murder.'

Lizzy expected the boy to run away, shocked by her brother's sharpness. Instead, he gave Charlie a quiet stare of disbelief. So as not to scare him, Lizzy extended her arm and said, 'I am Lizzy—Elizabeth Allen, and these are my brother and sister, Charlie and May. It's a pleasure to meet you.'

A look of fear and some arrogance stuck in the boy's eyes. As he shook her hand, a strange nervousness sent spiders down Lizzy's spine.

# Chapter 29

She should have been more afraid of Abel. He was a runaway from Holcombe House. But she wasn't scared. She knew real fear and had felt it when the vicious dog wanted to attack them. This boy didn't pose a threat.

'Where did you go the day when Mr Gains saw us?' Lizzy asked.

Abel hesitated. He took his time, making his mind up about something.

'I escaped through the door that brings me here. The one I found when I was playing.'

'A door?' Lizzy asked.

'Miss Inglestone said the house has secrets,' Munch said, 'and the older it is, the more it has.'

'Munch,' Lizzy said.

'I do not know what happens, but it always brings me here when I go through the door.'

His voice fell away when he saw Lizzy and Charlie's doubt, and he displayed his anxiety with jerking head movements.

May tugged at Lizzy's dress.

'It's not a game, Munch,' Lizzy whispered.

'But he said…'

'Stop it. Don't be silly.' She was about to say there was no door, but she didn't want to be rude with the boy so close.

'I found the door when I explored the manor,' he said to May.

'Oh yes? So, where is it then?' Charlie said.

'I cannot say, but I found it many months ago. The door was locked, but I managed to open it.' The pride was back in his voice, and he ignored the sarcasm in Charlie's voice.

As he spoke, May's eyes brightened. She was entranced.

'I explored it and saw the angry man. He asked me questions about who I am and where I come from. So, I showed him the ring as proof of my identity.'

Abel held out his hand. A gold ring with a radiant red diamond was on the middle finger. It was the same as the one Mrs Gains showed Lizzy.

'Is that the treasure?' May gasped in surprise.

'It is a fact in these parts. He who wears the ring is the master of Inglestone Manor. And I have it, so it follows that I am the master.'

'What did Mr Gains do?' Lizzy asked.

'He tried to steal my ring because he wanted to be the master. He insisted I take him to where I found it. But, I did not find the ring, I told him, it was given to me, as were the rest of my jewels.'

'Is there more?' Charlie asked.

'Many more, and they are all mine.'

'And there's a door?'

'I conclude. When I step through the door, I am transported here.' He spread his arms wide, indicating the manor and stood tall like a person of great importance. 'But I do not understand why it is in such a state. It was not how I left it this morning.'

Charlie openly laughed at him, and Lizzy prodded him in the back to be quiet.

Rather than being annoyed, Abel went to the window.

'When I look at the village, I see buildings I do not recognise, such as the red-brick one on the outskirts. I know not when they rose from the sod.' He sneered and curled his lips. 'It is such an ugly building.'

'That's Holcombe House,' Lizzy said.

'And that strange flying machine. It is indeed a new world.'

He stood upright with his back to them, gazing out of the window, his hands clasped together behind him and his legs spread wide. It was an odd stance for one so young.

'He's mad,' Charlie whispered.

'Shush,' Lizzy said, afraid Abel would hear.

'Well, he's hardly dressed like he's the master of any manor, ring or no ring,' Charlie said.

'Maybe he's in disguise,' May whispered.

Charlie frowned and reiterated his conclusion, 'As a hatter.'

Something came to Lizzy. The Gains's attempts to convince her the boy was dangerous made sense.

'He has found them,' Lizzy said in a hushed tone. 'The diamonds. Don't you see? That's why Mr Gains is chasing him. Nobody can find them because Abel has them.'

After twenty years of searching, Mr Gains must have been appalled when the boy found them, and an insane boy at that. All his efforts were in vain. Who knows what Abel would do with the gems? He could hide them like a squirrel hiding acorns, one here, one somewhere else, all in different places. He could take them back to Holcombe

House, give them away to his friends, or even throw them away. There was no telling what insane people do. Then what would Mr Gains have? Lizzy had no doubt what Mr Gains was capable of in his desire to steal the Inglestone Diamonds.

'You do not believe me, but I assure you, what I say is the truth,' Abel said to Charlie.

His sincerity and seriousness when he spoke, made everyone silent. He hadn't complained and had been polite throughout, even when Charlie laughed at him.

May had been ignored for too long. 'Can I say something?'

'If it's about treasure or games, no, Munch,' Lizzy said.

May huffed and grumbled aloud, 'No one ever takes me seriously.'

'That's because you're never serious,' Charlie said.

'Is that right, Mr La de da? Maybe Abel can show us the door, so we can see for ourselves, is all I wanted to say.'

'It's a good idea, Lizzy. Then we'd know for sure, wouldn't we? I bet he won't show us, though, because he's making it up.'

May's cheeks glowed with satisfaction hearing Charlie's approval and not detecting any of his usual scepticism. Abel seemed delighted. If proof was needed, he could show them. Lizzy was apprehensive. "The boy's dangerous," she remembered Mrs Gains saying. "He's a mean one and he'll do you harm." Her nervousness returned, and she wasn't sure she wanted to go anywhere with him.

Chapter 30

Lizzy was outvoted. The others were too excited to be held back. This was a real adventure. Abel took the Allens up the wide staircase and along the corridors to one of the more damaged parts of the manor. They picked their way through the debris-littered floor that creaked under each step until they gazed down a long, smoke-blackened passageway. It was lit by daylight streaming in through holes in the ceiling where the roof collapsed.

'It is a secret, so you must swear to tell no one.' Abel cautioned them.

They were happy to swear and crossed their hearts to affirm it.

Satisfied, Abel announced loudly, 'The door.' He flourished an extravagant bow.

Lizzy was confused and felt apprehensive. Charlie and May looked at each other, equally puzzled.

The corridor was narrow, extending twenty feet and ending at a solid wall of peeling wallpaper with a door hanging off its hinges. The door was like all the rest in the manor and didn't lead anywhere. Beyond it, they had an unrestricted view of the snow-covered countryside to the far horizon and the sky. Lizzy approached gingerly and told the others to stay back. The room beyond the door had collapsed into the one beneath and into the basement. It was a great big hole into nothing. One step through the door would end in a fatal drop onto the rubble two storeys below. She had the awful feeling that Abel could come up behind her and push her off the edge.

In her nervousness she wheeled around to look at Charlie and May—had they seen something she didn't? It was clear from their expressions that they saw exactly the same. By contrast, Abel's demeanour suggested otherwise.

Charlie put a hand across his mouth and sniggered. Lizzy was aware that Abel had taken a step back and a look of severity washed over his face. His brow had furrowed. May copied Charlie.

In a quiet voice, Lizzy said, 'Abel, this door doesn't lead anywhere,' She didn't want to upset the boy.

'It is there,' he insisted and pointed.

Lizzy's eyes followed his finger. Perhaps there was another door, concealed and hidden from view. But there was still only one door and the vast drop when she looked.

'There.' Abel insisted more forcefully. He was clearly irritated, especially as Charlie and May were laughing openly.

'This is my playroom.' Abel walked to the door. He was angry and shouting at them. 'There is my rocking horse and my soldiers. See?' He pointed inside.

When Lizzy looked, to be polite, the view was the same as before—open moors, snow and acres of sky.

'Are you playing a game with me? I do not like you making fun of me. It is not funny in the least.' Abel demanded,

'Nor is yours,' Lizzy said.

This wasn't funny anymore, and Lizzy felt the hairs at the back of her neck rising. It was true. The boy was insane. Before she could move away, Abel lunged.

He grabbed her wrist and dragged her towards the opening.

'Come, I will show you,' he said crossly.

'Let go of me. You're mad?' Lizzy screamed. She twisted her arm free and retreated several paces. Her shout silenced Charlie and May. The boy had seemed harmless, but things had taken a sinister turn. They looked terrified.

'Stop it!' she shouted again as Abel stretched his hand towards her again. 'Are you trying to kill me?'

She ushered her brother and sister away, suddenly afraid of the boy, and looked back in terror in case he was going to throw them over. Abel was staring at her in disbelief. As they left, he ran after them, shouting, 'Wait, please wait. I did not mean to frighten you. Please come back. Please, I am sorry.'

It took Lizzy several minutes before she was calm. By then, they were in the ballroom, and the boy stood away from them with his head bowed as if he'd been told off.

'Will they not be missing you?' Lizzy said sharply, trying to control her anger, 'They'll be sending someone to find you?'

'No, my father and mother are busy with Christmas.'

'Stop it.' Lizzy shouted. 'The asylum—where you live, surely they will miss you.'

'The asylum?' Abel gave her a quizzical look. 'I do not understand. I do not live in an asylum. Do you think me mad? What have I done to make you think that? I only wanted to be your friend.'

'What have you done? You almost killed me! That's what you've done?'

'When have I tried to kill you? How can you say that? I extended you the hospitality of my home. How dare you insult me.'

His temper rose, and his eyes narrowed. His movements were agitated to match the level of his shouting.

Lizzy's temper wasn't far behind. However, she felt Charlie and May's fear, and they looked to her for what to do.

Abel swung around and stood with his back to them. He took several deep breaths before his head dropped. Folding his arms, he was quiet. Lizzy gathered Charlie and May to go back to the lodge. However, she stopped when she heard the boy's sob and saw his shoulders heave. He was crying.

'I do not understand,' he whispered between his sobs and sniffles.

Lizzy didn't understand his ailment. At first, he seemed harmless, and it wasn't his fault that he'd lost his grip on reality. He seemed to either believe his claims or didn't know how dangerous the drop was. It was clear he really did see what he said—if only in his head. He was a very sick boy. He didn't look dangerous, just confused. In an instant, he'd transformed into a helpless child, a lost and lonely soul being pursued by Mr Gains for the gems. But the fact remained that he had tried to harm her— however inadvertently—and she would be sure to keep an eye on him. Even so, she felt sorry for him, one of Milly's Poor Souls from Holcombe House.

# Chapter 31

'We didn't mean to laugh at you. Really. We're sorry,' Lizzy said. 'We have a lovely lunch. Would you like to share it with us?' Away from the corridor with the door leading to disaster, she felt safer.

'It's not that lovely. It's only bread and cheese with pickles, but there's enough for all of us.' Charlie looked contrite.

'Please have some with us,' May said.

Abel turned around. He sniffed, straightened his clothes, ran his fingers through his hair and nodded.

They sat in a space between two windows, sheltering from the draught. Lizzy brought a small kitchen towel to use as a tablecloth. The food was a meagre amount for four, but she made it stretch.

'Why do they call you Munch?' Abel asked as May handed him a sandwich.

'Because she's always munching on something,' Charlie said.

'She could eat for England,' Lizzy said.

May returned their smiles and, to prove their point, took a large bite from her sandwich. Her cheeks puffed out, making Abel laugh.

The colour returned to his face, and he seemed content with them again.

The meal was happy and much better than eating at the lodge.

'When I grow up. I want to be an explorer. I will explore Africa and China and kill wild lions and tigers, but only if they attack me.' Abel smiled at them.

'I'm going to be a pilot,' May said. She ran circles with her arms spread like wings as everyone laughed, except Charlie.

'I'm going to be the pilot. You just copy everything I want to do,' he was annoyed.

'Well, I'm not going to be an explorer or a pilot,' Lizzy said before May could reply. 'I've jolly well had enough of this war. I might become a doctor.'

'Doctor Elizabeth Allen.' May and Charlie burst out laughing, and Abel joined in.

Lizzy wagged a finger. 'Just you see if I don't.'

The conversation went about in a friendly and comfortable way. The Allen's sighed when Christmas came up because they would be away from home. When Abel asked why Lizzy explained the evacuation. He didn't understand. But she thought news of the outside must be slow to creep into his small world where they didn't need evacuation.

'Daddy used to hide our presents in the cupboard under the stairs,' Charlie said. When he saw the look on May's face, he laughed. 'I saw him do it once, and he didn't see me. When I looked, I found them. Every Christmas, I had a peek to see what he'd brought—it was fun seeing your faces when you opened your presents, and I already knew what they were. Even Mummy's face when she opened hers. And I had to pretend I was surprised when I opened mine. But it was always a lovely present.'

'I didn't know that. You didn't tell me.' May said.

'He didn't tell anyone, Munch,' Lizzy said.

'You knew as well?' May's realisation made her moan to Abel, 'See, I told you, no one ever tells me anything.'

She pouted and folded her arms to show how cross she was. She announced that she would never speak to them again—ever.

'But you've got an early Christmas present,' Lizzy said.

Lizzy opened May's coat to show the prancing hare.

'That's beautiful, Munch.' Abel used her nickname.

'Miss Inglestone gave it to me,' May said. She was clearly proud. 'She said it would bring me luck.'

'I do not know Miss Inglestone. I think I would like her because she sounds like a kind person.'

'Can he, Lizzy? Can he meet her? Please, Lizzy?' May asked.

Lizzy wondered if it was a good idea. Abel had asked about Miss Inglestone on several occasions, but she'd deliberately not engaged, fearing it would upset him because he believed he was the master of the house.

She felt sorry for him. Holcombe House must be an awful place, and she didn't think he had a family of his own—even though he pretended he did. And Milly's words came back to her of how they treated the inmates.

She'd speak to Miss Inglestone about it. She'd know what to do. She wanted to help Abel, and with Mr Gains away, he'd be safe.

\*\*\*

Too soon, the light was fading, and it was time to go. They didn't want to leave Abel alone in the cold manor overnight, but he got frightened when they suggested getting Ted to take him back home. He made them promise not to. Saying goodnight, Abel bowed deeply. His thanks were sincere. When he reached the foot of the stairs, he stopped and turned back. He looked so young and vulnerable again when he asked them, 'Please do not tell anyone about seeing me. Promise me you will not.'

He made them cross their hearts, and he bounded up the stairs and away.

'Will he be alright?' Charlie asked.

Lizzy didn't answer. The ruined manor must be preferable to the awfulness of Holcombe House, especially if what Milly said was true.

Until she could sort out her thoughts, they had to keep him a secret. She feared for his safety, not only from the goings-on inside the asylum but from Mr Gains too.

# Chapter 32

When they got to the lodge, Ted was in the kitchen with a cup of tea in his hand. Lizzy was worried the policeman knew about them and the boy and hoped they hadn't been seen.

'Well then, everyone's present except Billy. Gone to Leeds on business, you say, Ede? I daresay, you can tell him when he gets back.' Ted said.

'What's happened?' Lizzy asked.

'Let's go and see Miss Inglestone, and I can tell you all together.'

Miss Inglestone was sitting in her chair. She smiled when the policeman held out his arms to her. She raised hers with her wrists together.

'Yes, it was me, officer. I confess. I murdered the vicar. Done away with the silly man with a mallet. Put the handcuffs on and carry me away.'

'We'll let you off this once. But mind, don't make it a habit. Hello, Miss Inglestone. It's been a while. How are you?'

'How do you think, Ted? I'm still here, aren't I?'

'Oh, he only takes the good ones, I hear. You'll go on

forever, I'm sure.' He laughed.

'What an awful prospect. Can you imagine that? Stuck like this forever. Ah, my little explorers. These are the ones who keep me sane, Ted. Did you have a good day, children?'

'It was splendid, Miss Inglestone,' Lizzy said.

'I hope you've not been playing in the manor.' Ted furrowed his brows.

'No, not us. I mean not inside, sir,' May said nervously, and her gaze fell to the floor.

'We walked around it. That's what May meant,' Lizzy said.

Ted nodded. Whether he believed her was something else.

Miss Inglestone smiled and winked at May. 'Now, what can we do for the constabulary?'

'It's just a routine call, really. It's like before. Three people's gone missing from Holcombe House. They've been away a good while now, and we're worried. There was no need for concern before, and I'm sure there's none now. They'll run around a bit, and when they get hungry, they usually come back—poor beggars. But they might look odd, that lot do, shaved heads an' hollow-eyed, they are. If you come across them, don't approach them. Tell me or one of the others at the station, and we'll take care of it.'

'Some more have escaped from the loony bin, have they?' Mrs Gains said sharply, already knowing they had.

'How's about a bit more charity, Ede. One has already turned himself in as I left to come here. That leaves two missing—an older one and a youngster. The boy's eleven years old, and the doctor's worried about him. It ain't their fault they're like that, Ede.' Ted said.

The Allens exchanged glances, and Mrs Gains sniffed and whispered, 'Him again.'

'Are they dangerous?' Lizzy asked.

'Dangerous? No miss. Not dangerous like they'll do you harm. More a danger to themselves. They just act strange, that's all. You know? Thinking they're Napoleon or Genghis Khan, and the like—delusional, they calls it.'

'Or master of the manor,' Charlie said under his breath.

Lizzy nudged him.

'Not dangerous, indeed? They better not be. I'd take me broom to them.' Mrs Gains huffed.

'As I said, give it a few more days, and they'll come

back, like always.'

'Aye, and in the meantime, while you're doing nothing, they'll be murdering someone, Ted Bates.'

'No one's being murdered, Ede. We'll search the outlying barns again. That's where they're most likely to be, probably in one of the abandoned cowsheds.'

'If you ask me, too many go missing from that place. And too often. They ought to close it down.' Mrs Gains folded her arms stiffly.

'Well, it's a good job no one's asking you. It's not for you or me to decide what they do to the place. We'll search the manor, Miss Inglestone. Don't worry if you see some unfamiliar faces out of that window of yours. Them German prisoners are going to help as well... I know, Ede,' he said before Mrs Gains could say anything. 'You don't like them. But they're willing to help, and we can use every bit of that we can get. We're shorthanded as it is.'

He turned to the children and, looking at May, gave her a penetrating stare that made her nervous.

'Now, my little pup. You ain't seen anybody out of the ordinary on your travels, have you?'

'We didn't see a boy.' May swallowed and shook her

head.

'What she means is we did see someone that looked strange. Towards the main road, didn't we, Lizzy?' Charlie glared at May.

Lizzy nodded. 'He was too far away for us to make out much.'

'Strange... but too far to make out. I see. When was this?' Ted asked.

'This morning, soon after we left—going towards the hills. I mean, he was going, not us.'

'Well, let me know if you see him again. You'll let Billy know to be on the lookout when he gets back, Ede?'

'Oh, aye. I'll let him know, alright.'

'Anyway. I hope all's well, Miss Inglestone. It's been a pleasure as always. I only wish I could stay longer and have a decent chat, but I've another stop to make. Thanks for the tea, Ede. You make a good cup, for sure. Little pups, mind what I said about playing in the manor.'

Lizzy nodded as the policeman and Mrs Gains left.

'So, Munch, tell me about the boy,' Miss Inglestone raised a hand to silence Lizzy. 'I might be old, Elizabeth Allen, but I am not decrepit yet. Now, what is it you did not want her to say in front of Ted?'

'We met one of the missing people from the asylum,' Lizzy said.

'It was Abel.' May added.

'He wasn't dangerous, was he Charlie? He didn't do anything nasty or even look like he would. He was just hungry, so we shared our lunch with him.' Lizzy prayed her brother wouldn't mention what really happened.

'He said he was an Inglestone,' Charlie said mischievously.

'Charlie,' Lizzy shouted.

'Blabbermouth,' May snapped.

'An Inglestone? Did he now?' The old lady smiled.

'He said lots of things,' Lizzy said.

'He had one of the special rings. And he said that made him master of the manor,' Charlie said.

'Shush, Charlie,' May said.

'No, I won't.'

'He said nothing of the sort,' Lizzy said.

'Now, May, while these two argue and can't get their stories straight, you tell me what happened.'

May glanced at Lizzy from the corner of her eye.

'He was wearing one of the treasures,' she whispered conspiratorially to Miss Inglestone. 'It was a ring.'

'Was it gold with a red stone?'

May nodded. 'And he knew about all the treasure because he said he'd found it and it was him wot hid it.'

'He did not,' Lizzy said.

'Two rings were made. They were unique, and it was a well-known tale that they were owned by the Inglestones, the masters of the manor. So, May, tell me more about him—this strange boy.'

May loved being the centre of attention, it loosened her tongue, as Miss Inglestone knew it would. May told her about the morning's events. Every so often, Lizzy or Charlie had to correct something May said, much to the girl's annoyance, as she wanted to tell the story. Miss Inglestone was smiling, clearly enjoying May's descriptive re-enactment.

'And did you see the secret door?'

May went quiet, remembering how he scared her, and Lizzy took over. She nodded but didn't say what the boy had done. 'It could have led into a playroom in the old days. Maybe Abel saw some toys or something before they all got destroyed. But the room wasn't there anymore. Miss Inglestone, should we tell the policeman about him?'

'What do you think, Lizzy?'

'It's just that Holcombe House must be an awful place for him to want to run away and be without food.'

'I remember it when I was young. I recall it was a workhouse then and was a dreadful place. Horrid tales were told about it. The *Spike*, they called such places. Nothing much has changed since it has become a hospital. Lizzy, you must help him. It is a frightening world for him, one he has no knowledge of. I think everything he sees is new and different now.'

'We'll see him tomorrow and take him some food and blankets. If he looks ill or something, we'll tell the policeman.'

'No child. Promise, you will tell me before you do that.'

The sharpness in Miss Ingelstone's voice surprised Lizzie. They promised, and Miss Inglestone said she was tired, but she had a happy smile. As they left, a strange feeling came over Lizzy. She couldn't explain it, but it had something to do with Miss Inglestone and the boy.

# Chapter 33

Supper was waiting in the kitchen, as was Mrs Gains. She was her surly self, busy making a point of ignoring them. If Lizzy was worried that Mrs Gains would say anything about her dismissal and her part in it, she needn't have been. Mrs Gains was her efficient self and no more. She waited for supper to be over and Charlie and May to leave before speaking to Lizzy about the boy.

'Don't even think about lying to me, missy. You've met him, haven't you?'

Lizzy gave a puzzled glance hoping to convince Mrs Gains she didn't know what she was talking about.

'Don't you give me that butter wouldn't melt look. Aye, you've seen him all right. You can't fool me. You might pull the wool over that beggar Ted's eyes, but not me, missy. He's about twelve years old. Strangely dressed, and he's always hiding and looking shifty. Oh, Aye. That little one was about to say so, wasn't she?' Mrs Gains smirked as she carried the dishes to the sink. She'd seen through Lizzy's pretence.

If Miss Inglestone and Mrs Gains saw through her story, Lizzy wondered if she'd managed to fool the policeman.

'You be careful. I know you don't believe me, and there's no love lost between us, but he's dangerous—all the loonies from Holcombe House are. Why do you think they're there in the first place? You mark my words he's up to no good.'

'I don't know what you mean.' Lizzy remembered how Abel tried to drag her into the chasm.

'Aye, you do, missy. I know all about him. I reckon he's hiding somewhere in the manor.'

'If you're so sure, why don't you tell the policeman where he is?'

'Maybe I will. Maybe I won't. Let's see what Billy says about it when he comes back. He might have a different take on it.'

'I'm sure he will.'

'So, he's found the jewels, has he?'

'What do you mean?'

'It's not as big a house as you think, missy,' Mrs Gains said before turning away to deal with the dishes.

As Lizzy left the kitchen, she saw a look of satisfaction on Mrs Gains's face. She appeared all-knowing. The memory of her looking down on them from the window that first morning, sprang to mind. Lizzy knew the housekeeper had eavesdropped on their conversation. It made her worried for the boy.

# Chapter 34

The next morning, Ede looked pleased with herself. She whistled as she made breakfast. This change in mood wasn't lost on Lizzy, who waited for the sarcastic remark or an evil look. She was surprised when none came. After being sacked, it wasn't the demeanour Lizzy expected.

When Charlie and May went to see Miss Inglestone, Lizzy stayed behind. She was uneasy about the woman's change in attitude. Mrs Gains left the kitchen, and Lizzy took the opportunity to make sandwiches for their lunch and wrapped them in greaseproof paper to put in her knapsack. That she'd made up four sandwiches, she knew did not escape the housekeeper's attention. She cringed, waiting for the inevitable telling off—it never came.

Lizzy was quiet on the way to the manor. They met Abel again, and they all seemed comfortable in each other's company. He was animated today. With Christmas so near, just shy of a week away, he spoke about how the manor was decorated. Charlie and May were up for the make-believe game and were happy to play along with him. Abel entertained them with thrilling stories about events in the rooms.

Lizzy stood back, still lost in thought.

The boy didn't look to be in any great hardship. He must have been hungry because he hadn't eaten since the day before, but he didn't look too cold or put upon. He must have found a sheltered place to sleep with some warmth, and he seemed safe. She was relieved that she wouldn't have to tell the policeman about him. But she was uneasy—he couldn't stay there indefinitely. Whatever happened at Holcombe House, he'd have to go back. She wondered how she'd feel, if what Milly said was true, and whether she'd have the courage to speak up.

If anybody found out he was hiding in the manor and they knew about it, how much trouble would they be in?

Abel teased and joked with them, and when lunch came, he was pleased with the simple meal. He had a mischievous look, not unlike the one May wore when she tried to keep a secret. He asked them to wait and left the room, and when he came back, he seemed nervous.

'Please accept this,' he said shyly.

He took a black object from behind his back. It opened as he fiddled, spreading wider from the base hinge into a lady's fan. It was richly decorated with a pattern of delicate peacock eyes and inlays of silver and gold filigree that traced the outline of the feathers in bright contrast to the dark greens and black of the background.

'You have all been so kind to me. I need to show my appreciation. Please accept it.'

He gave the impression of being unused to the way people gave gifts and unsure of its reception.

'My goodness,' Lizzy said.

'It's beautiful,' Charlie said.

May stood with her mouth open.

'But we can't. I mean, it's so expensive, and we don't have anything to give you back.' Lizzy was embarrassed by his extravagance.

'Please, it is just a small thing.' He pushed it forward.

When Lizzy took it, his face flushed. He was going to say something but stammered and gave up. He was clearly uncomfortable, and after an awkward silence, he ran back to the staircase. Lizzy shouted, 'Thank you.'

They were stunned and took turns holding the fan, feeling its weight, and trying it out in the frosty air. Abel, it seemed, had found many more things in his exploration of Inglestone Manor than was evident and had amassed a treasure trove. They were all thinking the same thing.

After days of fruitless searching, they had the perfect present for Miss Inglestone. They rushed back to the lodge.

# Chapter 35

Billy Gains looked like a dishevelled tramp beside the kitchen sink. His clothes were crumpled and creased, and he swayed unsteadily. He'd returned from Leeds earlier than expected and said he'd stopped off somewhere before getting to the lodge. His face was ruddy and unshaven, and he had an odour of stale beer. Mrs Gains was making tea, and when the Allens came in, their conversation stopped. Billy Gains gave Lizzy a bitter look through bleary eyes and splashed cold water on his face.

It was a shock to see Mr Gains back so soon. Without him, it had been a good few days, and depression settled over Lizzy. The belief that she was responsible for him losing his position weighed her down. The feeling that he had not been given the post he applied for only added more guilt.

They went to their bedroom, and Charlie and May flopped on their bed. Lizzy refused to be sad and give in. She'd had enough of being held hostage by Mr and Mrs Gains. The seed of rebellion that germinated a few days ago grew and was ready to flower.

'We'll need to wrap the fan,' she said as she struggled to take off her wellington boots and fell back on the bed.

Her words were met with silence, and she sat up.

'I said we'll have to wrap it.'

They didn't answer.

'Now, you two listen. We will not be depressed or gloomy, is that clear?'

'I thought he was gone forever,' Charlie said.

'Well, he hasn't. Now, where are we going to get wrapping paper from? We could go to the shop around the corner if we were in London. Did anyone see anywhere in the village?'

May puffed out her cheeks, blew out a breath, and shrugged.

'So, we're going to have to improvise.'

Sad eyes looked up at her.

'Oh, I swear I'll spank you in a minute,' Lizzy tried to sound like Susan.

'Just you try it.' Charlie pouted.

'Yeah. Just you try.' May parroted.

'We've had a few good days, haven't we? We are not going to let Mr Gains beat us. So, he's back—so what? We're still together, and that's what matters. And we've got a present for Miss Inglestone, even if we don't get any ourselves.' May glanced up in horror. 'Yes, May, we might not. Now, are we okay?'

She received two reluctant nods.

'Good. Now wrapping.'

'How about using the newspaper? We could find a nice page that hasn't got tanks and bombs on it.' Charlie said.

'Splendid idea.' Lizzy smiled.

'If I had my crayons, I could colour it and draw stars and stuff,' May said.

'That's more like it. At least we can wrap it, can't we?'

Lizzy went to find an old newspaper, and they combed the pages for some uplifting news that was suitable. They struggled to find anything that wasn't about the war and all the awful things in the world, so they settled on the sports reviews.

'We need some string,' Lizzy said.

When they'd wrapped the fan, they sat back to admire their handiwork.

What started off as a snigger turned into loud giggles. It looked pathetic, absurd even. The fan was too lovely to be in the middle of a page of black text and a picture of a football match.

'This won't do,' Lizzy said between giggles. 'This won't do, one bit. It looks like we're giving her a portion of fish and chips. Any ideas?'

May put on her serious face and stared at it before shaking her head. Charlie looked at it intensely, his head cocked to one side, chewing his bottom lip.

'I know,' Lizzy said and rummaged through the vanity's drawers, lifting clothes and turning things over until she found what she was looking for. It was one of May's red satin ribbons. They removed the fan, and she wrapped the ribbon around it and tied the ends into a bow.

'There. What do you think?'

They looked at it for a minute in consideration. Charlie and May gave a nod of approval. It looked better. The red ribbon was a vivid contrast against the dark green and black fan with its gold decorations.

'We should have a card as well. That's the proper way to do it.' Charlie said.

'We'll make one. We can use a page from my notebook, and Munch can write it. Though it might look more like a note than a card.'

Lizzy tore a page and gave May her fountain pen. After a discussion about what to write, May wrote in her best writing,

*To Miss Inglestone, from Lizzy, Charlie and May,*

*A very merry Christmas and a Happy New Year.*

*X X X.*

To make it personal, she drew a border of stars and her best attempt at holly leaves and berries. She did it with care and stuck out her tongue to aid her concentration. When it was finished, Lizzy folded the note in half and slipped it between the loops of the ribbon.

'Who's going to give it to her?' Charlie asked, already knowing the answer.

'Me, please,' May shouted in excitement.

The bedroom door opened, and it made them jump. Mrs Gains came in with some folded clothes.

'What's all the noise,' she said in her gruff manner. She put the clothes on Lizzy's bed and saw the fan. Lizzy tensed, and her smile dropped.

'So, what you got there, then?'

No one answered her.

'Nice. Where did you get that from?'

She took the fan and turned it in her hand.

'Cat got your tongues?'

'From the village,' Lizzy said firmly. She was annoyed that she allowed Mrs Gains to touch the fan without protest.

'The village, you say.'

Lizzy nodded.

'Which shop?'

Lizzy didn't answer, and in the heavy silence, May mumbled, 'One on the high street.'

Mrs Gains looked at the fan.

'It looks old. Must be from Mrs Banksworth's place. She sells a lot of bric-a-brac. I'll have to see if she's got another for me.'

'She doesn't,' May said, looking up quickly. She looked down just a fast. 'I mean, she only had one,' she mumbled.

Mrs Gains smiled.

'We don't know which shop it was,' Lizzy said. 'We don't know their names.'

'That's a nice crest on the handle. It always suggests class when you see a crest, don't you think?' Mrs Gains gave the fan back and left the room.

Lizzy looked at the traitorous letter '**I**' surrounded by laurel leaves imprinted in gold leaf on the handle. The same design was carved into the keystone above the manor's front door. Lizzy took a deep breath to calm herself.

'What did she mean by a crest, Lizzy?' Charlie asked.

Lizzy showed them the imprint.

'In the olden days, important people had a family crest. It was a sign or an image they put on stuff to show it belonged to that family. This must be the Inglestone's. She must know it and didn't believe that we bought it in the village.'

'Shouldn't I have said that Lizzy?' May looked as if she'd done something wrong.

'No, May, you did well,' Lizzy said.

'The nosey old ninny,' Charlie scowled.

'I think we should give this to Miss Inglestone now.' Lizzy thought the fan might go missing if they waited until Christmas, just like their money. Hiding it was pointless. 'In fact, let's go and see her.'

'Will we get presents?' May sat on the bed as if her legs wouldn't carry her to Miss Inglestone's room, and her eyes sunk to the floor.

Lizzy sat next to her and put her arm around her. 'I'm sure Mummy will have brought some, and I bet she'll keep them in the cupboard under the stairs like Daddy did. She'll keep them safe for us until we get back. Come on, Munch, we can surprise Miss Inglestone, and that will cheer us up.'

# Chapter 36

May quite liked giving presents—next to receiving them, so, by the time they reached Miss Inglestone's bedroom, she had come out of her sulk. With a regained sense of humour, she sat on the edge of the bed in delight. The fan was behind her back. Keeping secrets was never May's forte, and the smile on her face gave her away.

When she produced the present after Lizzy said how grateful they were for Miss Inglestone's kindness, the old lady gasped, and her face shone. She held out a trembling hand, read the makeshift card in silence, and undid the bow. She admired the fan with noises of approval but said nothing else. She gave each a kiss and a hug and then was silent in thought.

'This belonged to my grandmother. It was one of a pair. I have the other here.'

She opened the bedside drawer and took out an identical fan. Her eyes were watery, and she swallowed to clear her throat.

'One was lost many years ago.' Her voice almost broke, and she had to stop for a second. 'And here it is again.'

May was talking too fast, and it was left to Lizzy to make sense of her ramblings. She told her how Abel gave it to them, and they thought it was the perfect gift for their guardian.

'Is the boy well?' Miss Inglestone asked.

Lizzy nodded. 'But, Miss Inglestone, the nights are so cold. I worry about him.'

'I know you worry. Elizabeth, I feel that he is all right and quite happy. What strange times these are, Elizabeth. This war and the great changes it will bring. We need something of the past to cling to. Something sure and constant that does not change. So, tell me, Munch, what do you think of him? Do you like Abel?' She held the fan closer to her breast, and May didn't need to answer. 'You like him. I can see that. As do you, Charles. I am sure he likes you all as well—how could he not like such sincere children?'

# Chapter 37

That night, Lizzy woke from her sleep several times. On the last occasion, there was a crash followed by a long silence. In the empty quiet, she was wide awake, and it was only one o'clock. She listened to her brother and sister breathing before loud whispers under the window startled her. Mr Gains and his wife were arguing in the garden. When she peeked out, she saw them huddled in their coats. A thin sliver of yellow light fell on them from the kitchen door, and their breath was visible in the cold air.

'Are you mad?' Mrs Gains puffed on a cigarette, and the end glowed bright in the darkness.

'I've come too far, Ede—I ain't backing down. Fortune favours the brave, isn't that what they say?'

'They say a lot of things that don't make sense, Billy.'

'What do you want? To be a pauper all your life? Clearing up after the likes of her? Is that what you want? It'll be all over in the new year, Ede—then we're gone. We'll be on our tod then.'

'Aye, and whose fault was that?'

'Now you blame me? You didn't complain when you

wore your new hat, did you?'

Mrs Gains snorted and took a deeper drag from her cigarette.

'I know where he is now, Ede, and I want him. Wherever he's stashed the jewels, I'll find them. I ain't seeing twenty odd years go to waste because of some loon.' He took a deep swig from a bottle of beer. 'It's rightfully mine—I'm the one who sweated for it.'

'And he's the one that got it,' she said sarcastically.

That made Mr Gains angrier, and he took another drink.

'Do you still think it's worth it, Billy?' She dropped the cigarette on the floor and ground it into the stone. 'All its brought us is unhappiness. You're the laughing stock of the village. They talk behind our backs. But you don't hear them, do you?'

'I don't give a fig what they say. Yes, it's worth it.'

'I'm not sure anymore.'

'I've been looking for those things ever since Old Inglestone died. The old beggar. Things like that's only good for the cash you get for them, otherwise, they're just pretty trinkets. People can say what they want, but when I get the diamonds, I'll be someone. Are you still with me,

Ede?'

'In for a penny,' she said after a few seconds of hesitation.

'What's wrong?'

'What if he doesn't tell you? Have you thought about that?'

He scowled, muttering something that Lizzy couldn't hear.

'You've changed Billy,' Ede whispered.

'Things have changed. Those kids have seen to that. She ain't herself anymore, either. Aye, I saw the fan. You're right, she got another the same.'

'You'll get caught one of these days, sneaking into her bedroom.'

'Fat chance. She sleeps like the dead.'

He drained the bottle, went in and came back with another.

'Give me the ring,' he said.

Mrs Gains took the ring off her chain and gave it to him. He looked at it, slipped it on his little finger twisting his hand to see the diamond glimmer.

'It's late,' Mrs Gains said. 'You coming to bed?'

He looked at the nearly full beer bottle and shook his

head.

'I'm going to get him. You'll see. Now that I know where he is.' He tipped the bottle and took a long draught, wiping his mouth and belching, before staring into the dark. 'Time's short. They'll pull the place down when she goes, and everything will be lost forever. It'll all be for nothing.'

Lizzy watched him until the cold forced her back under the blanket's warmth. She lay awake worrying about Abel and wished they'd never come. What she would give to be in their small house again, to wake up in her own bed and hear her mother or Susan calling them for breakfast.

# Chapter 38

There was a strange atmosphere in the kitchen the next morning. The sneers and curt remarks were gone, Mrs Gains's usual greeting replaced by an awkward silence that hung heavily in the fuggy air. A peculiar feeling made Lizzy shiver as she watched Mrs Gains with dark curiosity and saw her stiffen when her husband came in.

Bill Gains looked as if he'd just woken up. He was even more dishevelled than usual. He was quiet. He took the shotgun off its hook and dipped his hand in a coat pocket. Pulling out a handful of shotgun cartridges, he stuffed them back in after counting them. Then, taking a parcel of sandwiches from his wife, he left.

Lizzy ignored Charlie's look. She was worried, and her restless mind refused to let go of the idea that Abel was in danger. As she collected the dishes, Mrs Gains took the plates from her, but not in her usual way. She did so calmly, which added to the strange atmosphere.

'Why don't you lot go to the village today,' Mrs Gains said. 'There's bound to be some celebrations. Last year, them German lads put up a Christmas display in the square. Nowt much mind, but nice if you like that kinda thing. Why don't you see if they've done it this year?'

Her voice was earnest, and she didn't look at them when she spoke.

'We might do that, Mrs Gains,' Lizzy said. 'Thank you, I'm sure it'll be nice.'

'Aye, it usually is.'

'But we thought we'd go to the manor.'

Mrs Gains looked around. Lizzy thought she'd sneer or make a rude remark, and everything would be back to normal. But she said, 'Aye, well, if you must, sobeit.'

It was odd to hear the concern in her voice.

'That was strange,' Charlie said when they left the kitchen.

'I know. She and Mr Gains had some words last night. I heard them. He looked like he slept in a barn, didn't he?'

As they walked to the manor, Lizzy picked up the pace and her anxiety wasn't lost on Charlie.

'What did Mr Gains say?' Charlie asked.

'Just that he knew where Abel was. I think we should warn him to go back to Holcombe House.'

'No, Lizzy,' May said. 'They'll hurt him. Milly said she's seen them doing things to them.'

'Oh, May, I think he's in more danger here. I'm very worried. We should tell the policeman. He'll know what to do. After we see Abel, we'll go and see Ted.' Things were coming to a head. She felt it keenly.

'Won't Abel be annoyed?'

'Everyone's going to be annoyed—at least with me. But it's too late to worry about that. We'll tell Abel what we're going to do and see what happens.'

'We can't tell on Abel,' May said. 'We promised.'

'Mr Gains will hurt him if he finds him.'

'He hasn't found him yet,' May said.

'I think he has.'

'But we crossed our hearts, Lizzy.'

'I know.'

'He says he knows where to hide so Mr Gains will never find him. He'll be all right, and Milly said they'll hurt him.'

'Stop that, May. I know what Milly said. Abel's not safe anymore, can't you see?'

'Where shall we start looking?' Charlie asked as they reached the pillars.

'In the ballroom.'

They crossed the path, and a sinking feeling

overwhelmed Lizzy. She was hot with worry—the manor was a huge place, and he could be anywhere. They couldn't even shout for him in case Mr Gains was nearby.

She heard a dog barking inside the manor.

Charlie and May were rooted to the ground.

When Lizzy beckoned them on, they came apprehensively. Lizzy hadn't thought it through. In her rush to warn Abel, she'd forgotten about her brother and sister's safety. 'You two, go back to the lodge. Now. Go on.'

They stood their ground.

'What're you going to do?' Charlie asked.

'Find Abel. Now, go back and take May with you.'

'I'm not leaving you,' Charlie said.

'I'm not leaving either,' May agreed.

'Sabre's in there,' Lizzy pleaded. 'I can't look after you and Abel.'

Charlie looked around. When he heard the bark again, he trembled but turned to Lizzy with a determined look. 'I'm not leaving you.'

May drew closer to Charlie and shook her head—she was staying.

Lizzy was horrified. 'Stop it. Go back to the lodge or

the village; find the policeman. Don't you understand? It's dangerous.'

'No, Lizzy, we have to find Abel,' May said.

'Please, go back!' Lizzy shouted.

'No! You said Mr Gains will hurt him. He's got a gun.'

'May, Charlie, please help me out here.'

Lizzy was stunned. She wanted to shout at them, as she knew pleading wouldn't help. Either they went on together, or they abandoned Abel and all went back to the lodge. She couldn't take the chance with Sabre there. She took their hands and walked away—the promise she made to her mother had to come first.

The crack of a shotgun pierced the air, freezing them to the spot. Then a second came from inside the building.

'Abel,' May shouted and pulled free. Turning on her heels, she ran full pelt towards the manor before Lizzy could do anything.

'Stop. May, Stop.' Lizzy shouted and took off after her.

It was too late. The little girl was through the front door and charging towards the barking. She ran through the hallway. Climbing the stairs, she almost tripped but somehow kept her balance. She was in a blind panic. In a moment, she was running towards the corridor where Abel had shown them his secret door, and as she turned the corner, she stopped, petrified at the sight before her.

Bill Gains held Abel's wrist, dragging him across the floor with a wild look of triumph in his eyes. The boy kicked and struggled against the vice-like grip, while behind him, next to the door that led nowhere, Sabre snarled viciously.

'Let me go,' Abel shouted and was greeted by Mr Gains's wild laughter.

When he saw the Allens, he smirked and pulled Abel forward, lifting him by his wrist as if he was a prize turkey. He was triumphant.

'I've got him. I've got the beggar. I said I'd get him.'

May took a step forward, and Lizzy pulled her back.

'Leave him alone.' Lizzy shouted. She wanted to hit Mr Gains, but the snarling dog was standing beside him. Its dark eyes were set on her. 'He doesn't mean anyone harm. Leave him alone.'

'Not this time, missy. He's got some questions to answer first.'

'Let me go,' Abel struggled.

'We'll tell the policeman,' Charlie shouted.

'Tell who you want, mister. Tell the whole bloomin' world.' He glared at Charlie, who shrank back in fear. 'But you do, and I swear I'll do him a mischief—I swear I will.'

Lizzy found her courage. Buoyed up by her anger, she stepped forward and ignored Sabre. She swung her fist, and Mr Gains burst out laughing. Her blow had hardly troubled him.

'Is that the best you can do?' he sneered.

He pushed her away, sending her clattering into Charlie and May and they all sprawled onto the floor.

'Don't hurt him,' Charlie screamed.

Ignoring their shouts, Mr Gains dragged the boy down the stairs, across the foyer, and into the snow.

'Come on, Sabre,' he shouted, and the dog bounded up, but it turned its head to growl at the Allens.

As much as Abel struggled by digging in his heels, biting and scratching, he was no match for the man. Madness had overtaken Mr Gains. By the time they reached the lodge, the fight was gone from Abel, and Mr Gains pushed the kitchen door open. He swung the boy inside with a heave, throwing him sprawling onto the stone floor to the surprise of his wife.

'Lord Almighty, Billy,' she said when she saw the boy's frightened face. 'What have you done?'

# Chapter 39

Bill Gains was a man possessed. He'd lost all reason when he swore at his wife, a bitter curse that made her lurch backwards. Dragging Abel, he pushed him into the cellar and slammed the door. He locked the boy in and came back laughing wildly and wiping his sweaty, jubilant face on his sleeve.

'For God's sake—answer me.' Edith Gains said.

'I've got him. I've got the beggar.'

Mrs Gains looked horrified. She rushed to the window, fearful somebody might be watching and sat down. Her eyes couldn't settle and flicked between the cellar, her husband and the children—a cold fear had gripped her, and she trembled.

The children were on her, all talking at the same time, pleading with her, imploring her to do something, but she barely heard them.

'Billy, what have you done?' she mumbled.

'Please, Mrs Gains, help him,' Lizzy screamed.

May had hold of her arm, and Charlie begged her to help.

'Shut up,' she barked at them. 'I can't think.' She put

her hands over her ears.

Billy Gains clasped a bottle of beer in his hand, smirked and sniggered at everyone, then took a deep draught.

'This is out of hand. Have you lost your mind?' Ede shouted.

'I've got him like I said I would.'

'Billy, what'll happen next?'

'Don't go soft on me.' He glared at his wife. It was a dark look, and she turned away in fear. 'Nothing will happen, not if he tells me what I want to know.'

May burst into tears and screamed, 'I'm going to tell Miss Inglestone.'

She ran to the door, but Bill Gains was too quick and grabbed her.

'No one's telling anybody anything if they know what's good for them. And you ain't telling either.' He swung May back, and Lizzy caught her before she fell. 'He stays, do you hear? Stays until he talks. You'd better think twice about telling anyone or by God, I swear I'll do the little beggar harm. I swear I will.'

He loomed over them in the dark kitchen, like a black shadow, taking up the space. His face was creased with menace.

'You think anyone will miss him? Why do you think they locked him up in that place? It's because he's a loony, crackers—off his bloody rocker, that's why, and no one's gonna give a tinker's damn for him.' He dropped his voice to a rasping whisper and narrowed his eyes. 'If anyone tells anything, just remember I can put him somewhere where he'll never be found. Ever. Even if they search all year and a day. Now shut up and stop your bawling.'

'Billy, it isn't right. You can't do this.'

'In for a penny, you remember? You said that wife, you said it!'

He slapped his hand on the table with a loud clap, and when he lifted it, there was a gold ring. He put his left hand beside it with an identical ring on his small finger. The two red diamonds winked in the light.

'He had it on.' His eyes widened as he looked at the rings. 'I couldn't believe my luck when I saw it. You tell me where the little thief got that? He knows about the jewels, and he's going to tell. If he knows what's good for him, he'll tell Uncle Billy.'

'Billy, you've not thought this through.'

'Oh, I have, Ede.'

'No, you have not, Mr Gains.' Standing like a frail ghost at the door behind him, Miss Inglestone wore an angry look. 'Let the boy go.'

The kitchen was quiet. Bill Gains was shocked, and the grin left his face. He took a breath and was calm and sure.

'I don't believe I will if it's all the same to you, Miss Inglestone.'

'He does not know the whereabouts of the jewels. No one does. They are lost, sold, gone. Now, let him go.'

'That's where you're wrong old lady. He does. Now, why don't you toddle back to bed while I ask him kindly like.'

'I swear if you harm him…'

'You'll do what, Miss Inglestone? What're you going to do, Dorothy? Fire me? You've already done that. Keep back me wages? As if I care. Beat me with your riding crop? Isn't that what your old dad would have done?'

The menace in his voice made Mrs Gains shiver, and the children huddled together.

'I'm through taking orders from the Inglestones. You lot have had your day. A mad boy, an old woman and some London brats—what're you going to do? Tell Ted how naughty I've been? There's worse things happening for him to worry about someone's feelings getting hurt. And the boy's dangerous. He tried to kill me.'

'Liar,' Miss Inglestone screamed.

'Who's going to believe you? It's his word against mine, and he's crazy.'

The old woman shook with anger, and Bill Gains sneered at her.

'Are you going to stand there and do nothing, Edith? Billy will go to jail for this. You do know that?'

Mrs Gains didn't move.

'She knows which side her bread's buttered,' Mr Gains said. 'Now toddle along, old woman. I'll give him to the police when I'm done, and they can lock him up for good, someplace where he can't do a runner.'

'I want to see him,' Miss Inglestone demanded.

'But, you're not giving the orders anymore. I am.'

'I will see him,' she said firmly.

'You can't order me about anymore…'

'Let her see him. For God's sake, Billy. What harm will it do?' Mrs Gains said. 'I'll get her to bed afterwards.'

Bill Gains took another drink.

'No skin off my nose. She can have until I finish my beer. Then I want words with him. And you lot, get off to your room. And don't think about running off to the village. I ain't in the mood for tricks.' Lizzy glared at him, and he glared back with equal hatred. 'And you try hitting me again, missy, and I'll see that you're sorry.' he pointed a finger at her.

'Leave it be, Billy,' Edith said.

Mrs Gains shepherded them out of the kitchen. Lizzy tried to speak, but she refused to listen, and when they reached the cellar door, she let Miss Inglestone in. As they went upstairs to the bedroom, Bill Gains was watching.

'I ain't seen him like this before,' Edith Gains said. 'You lot keep out of his way, and you'll be okay. I'll calm him down.'

'Please, Mrs Gains,' Lizzy said. 'Help Abel. He hasn't done anything wrong.'

'Just mind what I said and leave it. There's nowt I can do.'

Charlie and May pestered Lizzy. But Lizzy sat on her bed and couldn't comprehend what had happened. She heard the key turn in the lock and Edith Gains saying, 'It's for your own good.' She tried the handle, but it was locked. Lizzy banged on the door and hollered, 'Let us out,' but to no avail.

# Chapter 40

Charlie and May were looking at her. They were scared and ready to burst into tears. She felt like crying too. But, she was the eldest and the one they looked to for courage and hope. She went to the window and peered out. The drop to the ground was too far, they couldn't jump. The door was the only way out. When she turned back. May and Charlie were looking at her, silent and frightened.

Lizzy was lost. She wondered what Susan would do. In times of trouble, she'd break into song and make everyone laugh or tell stories about her old man and take their mind off their troubles. Her mother would take Lizzy aside and explain things, treating her like a grown-up. But being a grown-up was the last thing she felt like. She was helpless.

'I don't know what to do,' she whispered.

'You'll think of something,' Charlie said.

Lizzy managed a weak smile.

'Will Abel be okay?' May asked.

Lizzy knew what Mr Gains was capable of. The look in his eyes when he had Abel, haunted her.

'I don't know. Maybe Mrs Gains will talk him out of hurting him.' Though she didn't believe it—it was just something to say, to give her space to think. 'We have to get out of here and find the policeman.'

May glanced at the window.

'No, it's too high.'

'They can't keep us locked in here forever,' Charlie said.

But forever wasn't the point. It was the next few hours that mattered.

'What if Abel doesn't know where the jewels are?' May said.

They were Lizzy's fears too. She dreaded Mr Gains's retribution if he thought the boy was lying.

'Dear God, I hope he does,' she whispered.

The house was quiet. There were a few minutes of shouting, and now nothing. Lizzy listened but heard little. Her imagination took over. She saw all sorts of horrible things happening to Abel, and her concern grew, making her desperate to get out. But the door was solid.

They sat as midday went by and afternoon came. Lizzy tried the door, hoping that by some strange miracle, it would open.

They heard Mr Gains's angry voice, but they couldn't make out the words. Once, they saw him in the garden, smoking and unsteady on his feet. He almost fell, and he looked at whatever tripped him and cursed. He was drunk and seemed dishevelled, his shirttail hanging out and his unshaven face ugly with rage.

May got up and banged on the door, shouting to be let out. Lizzy took her aside and gave her the biggest hug she could. Sobbing, May curled up on her bed and fell asleep, while next to her, Charlie was quiet.

As the light faded, the room got dark.

Lizzy waited. Before long, her anger faded and was replaced by a simmering hatred. When she closed her eyes, she saw herself striking Bill Gains, a firm, resounding, crashing punch and him falling down, struck by the blow. But she had tried that, and all he did was laugh.

Mr Gains was right. No one would miss Abel. Just the asylum and she wondered if they would care. Mr Gains had searched for the jewels for so long, and now he was this close, he would never stop—because nothing else mattered.

Lizzy dozed. She'd hardly slept the night before. She

curled up and drew the blanket around her as the room froze. Soon she fell into a dreamless sleep.

# Chapter 41

Lizzy had no idea how much time had passed when she woke with a start. The room was dark, and someone was turning the key. She sat up as the door opened just enough to let the sliver of light that fell across the threadbare carpet. Miss Inglestone entered and whispered, 'Shush, child,' with her finger on her lips. She carried a torch. Across the room, Charlie and May stirred awake.

'Elizabeth, you must help him.'

Her ashen face was contorted with worry, and she was breathing heavily. She seemed to have shrunk into herself.

'He must get back to the manor. It is imperative. I am so afraid. I am fearful of what Mr Gains will do to him if he stays here. And so is Abel.'

She seemed on the point of tears.

'Oh, there is so much to tell, I scarcely know where to begin, but I promise I will tell you everything when he is safe.'

'Tell me what, Miss Inglestone?' Lizzy wiped the sleep from her eyes and trembled, but not from the cold.

'This is a key to the cellar—take it,' she placed an old iron key into Lizzy's hand along with the torchlight. 'Mr Gains is sleeping. He has drunk too much. But I don't know where Edith is. Set Abel free. Get him to the manor where he will be safe. You must trust me. He will be safe there.'

'He wasn't before.'

'He will be now, child.'

Lizzy took the key, confused by what Miss Inglestone said. Charlie and May had resolve on their faces, and she said, 'No, you're not coming.' The look she received told her that they wouldn't leave her, and it was pointless to argue. Then how could she leave them with Mr Gains in the house, especially if he discovered Abel missing? It was best that they come.

They crept along the corridor on tip-toes, fully aware of how alarmingly the floorboards squeaked, and afraid it would alert the Gains.

Lizzy looked over the bannisters to see if anyone was lurking. She slipped down the stairs. In the half-light, she found the cellar door, and as everyone kept watch, she opened it. Her heart thumped as the key grated and scraped. The lock opened with a snap that caused her to glance fearfully towards the kitchen.

For a second she held her breath. All she could hear was the guttural snores of Mr Gains, fast asleep. She pushed the door open.

Lizzy saw a pile of clothes in the corner move. It gave a soft moan, and when the torchlight fell on it, a hand emerged and shielded its sight from the harshness of the glare. The face was bruised, and its eyes, quick and bright, found Lizzy's and looked at her in fear. He retreated into the darkness. Lizzy was horrified, and a wave of rage surged through her.

'What has he done to you?' she whispered. She couldn't believe the pitiful boy in front of her was the person they had played with. She knelt beside him, and he, recognising her, grasped her hand tightly and smiled at the sight of a friendly face. Lizzy wanted to say more, but the words choked in her throat, strangled by the rising tide of anger and hatred for Bill Gains. She helped Abel get up. He could still stand, though he was unsteady.

'I didn't tell him?' he said in a hoarse whisper.

'We must go,' Lizzy said, 'lean on me.'

'It belongs to me, and he's not going to get it.'

'Be quiet, Abel. We must go. You've got to go back to

Holcombe House for your own good. He won't dare try and hurt you when you're back there.'

'No. I need to go to the manor.'

'Leave the jewels. We have to get you to safety.'

'The manor.'

'Take him to the manor, Elizabeth,' Miss Inglestone whispered.

'But Miss Inglestone, it's not safe.'

Both were firmly set, and she agreed and was frightened and too tired to argue further. When they emerged, the sight of the bruised boy shocked May into tears. She was about to sob, but Charlie put a hand across her mouth.

'Don't. Mr Gains is asleep. We mustn't wake him. Please don't cry.'

'It'll be all right, Munch. We're going to the manor, and Abel will be safe there. He knows all the hiding places. Mr Gains will never find him. Be brave, Princess Allenova,' Lizzy said.

May wiped her eyes and quietly blew her nose on her sleeve. Abel gave her a smile of triumph.

'Go now,' Miss Inglestone whispered.

Abel's eyes caught hers. It lingered—a puzzled look

on his face and a kindly one on hers. He moved towards her, but she raised her hand.

'Go. Be safe. There is nothing more to explain. Now go.'

Lizzy couldn't interpret the strange look they exchanged and intended to ask its meaning.

Like thieves in the night, they crept towards the sound of snoring coming from the kitchen. When Lizzy peeked through the crack in the door, she saw Mr Gains, his head on the kitchen table, wheezing, with an empty beer bottle beside him.

To her horror, Mrs Gains was awake. She was standing by the sink, looking at her. The housekeeper was pale, and she dropped the cigarette she was smoking to the floor, grinding it out with the sole of her shoe.

Lizzy's blood was up. She felt the rising tide of hatred swelling inside her, making her clench her fists around the torch she'd swing if needed. She gritted her teeth in grim determination. Edith Gains, though, turned around, and stood with her back to them. She gazed out of the kitchen window into the black night beyond the glass.

On tip-toes, they filed past the sleeping figure of Mr Gains, and Lizzy opened the door.

Bill Gains woke. The hint of a breeze from the open door, a slight movement, or the feeling of someone walking on his grave disturbed him. His confused face lifted from the crook of his arm. He struggled to make sense of what was happening, his limbs were stiff, paralysed into stillness. His eyes caught Lizzy's. He looked puzzled before understanding washed over his face.

He stood up fast, knocking the chair away with a growl.

'Run,' shouted Miss Inglestone. 'Run!'

# Chapter 42

As Bill Gains moved, Miss Inglestone struck him with her cane. He stumbled, and she hit him again as his hands rose up to shield his head.

'Get after them, Ede,' he shouted.

Edith Gains stood resolutely still.

Another blow fell on him. He growled like an animal, and as Miss Inglestone raised her cane for the next crash, he struck her. A firm blow sent her reeling against the wall. She fell to the ground, a tangled heap of bony legs and arms sprawled across the cold floor.

'You've killed her,' Edith Gains screamed in horror and ran to the old woman.

Her husband stood over the twisted figure on the ground. His face red with rage. 'No one hits me, no one,'

Miss Inglestone's eyes opened. She glared at the dark figure.

'If father were alive, he would whip you like a dog.'

Bill Gains pushed his wife away and leant close to the hurt woman. Pleasure curled his lips into a sickly smile.

'Aye, he tried that once,' he whispered loudly. 'And look where that got him. I wanted just one of those bloody gems. No more. He'd plenty—he wouldn't have missed one. He'd taken that ring of his off and dropped it. I were holding it, and he grabbed it back and accused me of stealing it. He thought he'd give me a hiding. I told him to back off, but he wouldn't. So, I hit him like I did you, Miss Bloody Inglestone.'

'Billy? What are you saying?' Edith Gains pulled at his shoulders.

'Knocked his head off, I did. Killed the old beggar dead with one blow.'

'You killed him?' Miss Inglestone gasped at the confession. 'Dear God. He was kind to you.'

'Kind? He was never kind to anyone.'

'He looked out for you when your father died. He gave you a job.' Miss Inglestone's voice trembled.

'Stable boy? Call that a job?'

'He cared about you.'

'Cared. What the hell do you know about anything? When did you ever have to scrape for a living? Everything you've had was given to you on a plate. You've never had to work for a penny in your life.'

'Billy, stop.' Edith Gains was frozen as if caught in a hard frost.

'I killed him. Aye, it were me that did him. He always said he felt responsible for me. What did he mean if he couldn't let me keep that one bloody ring? He'd no need of it.'

Bill Gains shook in anger. He gazed behind him through the open door.

'Now, I'm going to find that boy, and when I do, he tells me where he's hidden the rest.'

'He will never tell you,' Miss Inglestone said weakly.

'Then I'll finish what I started and make sure I burn that damn place down properly this time. If he's hiding there, I'll burn him out.'

'You set his house on fire?' Edith Gains pulled away as if she saw him for the first time. 'You did that, Billy Gains?'

'Aye. That were me an' all. Now you know. Me. I did it. Me—Billy Gains the stable boy. I were the one.'

He pulled her to him, and Edith Gains looked at his unpleasant face in terror.

'Make your mind up, Ede. Whose side you're on, them or me?'

She twisted free and edged away.

'You leave me alone, Billy Gains. You leave me be.

Do you hear me? I don't know you.'

He sneered and scowled, 'You two deserve each other,' and pushed Edith. She tumbled against Miss Inglestone, and they lay together on the ground. He swung on his heels. Stopping only to take the shotgun off the hook, he stormed out of the kitchen.

Edith touched the old woman's face and gasped in relief to feel a spark of life there.

'I'll get help, Miss Inglestone. I'll fetch the doctor. Oh, please don't die.'

As she rose, Miss Inglestone grasped her hand.

'Daddy said he could change Billy. He just needed to feel loved and wanted. That is why he helped him—it was his duty to help make him the best man he could be.'

'Save your strength, Miss Inglestone.'

'Poor, Daddy,' Miss Inglestone whispered, her tears mingling with the blood on her cheeks. 'Daddy, where are you?' she clutched her heart. 'Yes, I promise. I will not forget.' She stared through glassy eyes as if seeing a ghost in front of her. 'I promise—Elizabeth, Charlie and Munch,' she grasped Edith Gains's arm. 'The children will arrive in December, Ede, just as he said. We must get things ready for them. I've kept my promise, Ede. I have.'

'Said they would? Who said they would? What do you mean, Miss Inglestone?'

The old lady closed her eyes. She was unconscious.

Edith placed her coat over Miss Inglestone to keep her warm and rushed out to the village. In the moonlight, she could just make out the figure of her husband walking on a march towards the manor. His head was down, and he carried a can of petrol. Behind him, Sabre barked into the night.

## Chapter 43

Abel's strength failed when the children got to the manor, and he collapsed. Despite Lizzy's urgings, he couldn't move and rested on the ground. Behind them, they heard the sharp bark of Sabre somewhere in the darkness and, every now and then, the booming voice of Bill Gains.

'You must try,' Lizzy implored him. She could see the fret in May and Charlie's faces and the expectation that Sabre would appear at any moment. It made them look like trapped prey.

Abel stood up.

'I must get to the door. Then we can all be safe.' His eyes wandered aimlessly.

Lizzy shook her head in frustration. She wanted to shout at him that this was no time for his fantasies. Abel was determined, and nothing would sway him. They had to find a place to hide. Bill Gains's voice was nearer.

They climbed the staircase and felt their way along a dark corridor. Gains had changed direction, and Sabre was barking somewhere ahead of them. Lizzy used the torch sparingly, afraid Mr Gains would see the light. Instead, she felt her way to a room, and they crouched low behind its walls and waited for the moonlight to show them the way. She felt May's hand tremble in hers as the moon reappeared.

'Be brave,' Lizzy whispered. May was like a little bird trying to make herself look small.

Lizzy wished she'd made Charlie and May stay behind, this was madness. At least she should have sent them to find the policeman. An overwhelming feeling of guilt invaded her mind. Things were happening too fast, and she couldn't think quickly enough. But how could she have let them stay in the same house as Bill Gains, knowing what he was capable of? Yet, here they all were, in even greater danger. What else could they do? There were no choices left. They had to go on.

'Come out, come out, wherever you are,' she heard Bill Gains sing-song voice in the darkness. He jeered, and Sabre barked. 'You ain't going nowhere, boy. Not until you tell me where they're at.'

'He's mad,' Charlie whispered.

'Can you smell smoke?' Lizzy asked.

The distinct smell of smoke was in the air. Lizzy heard the crackle of burning wood. She looked into the hallway and saw the glow of a fire, and through a hole in the floor, she saw Mr Gains adding more timber. She saw the madness in his eyes as flames jumped into life around him, catching on the long-dried wallpaper and running up the walls. He wheeled around in a circle, almost falling down in his drunken lurch. Insanity gripped him, and he raised his shotgun and fired wildly, losing both barrels, and Sabre bounded away, barking in the direction of the shots.

Lizzy gasped. Mr Gains was systematically setting the manor alight. He had lost all sense of reason.

'We have to leave, now,' she urged Abel. The boy didn't budge. He had slumped on the floor and she pulled him. He refused to rise. 'We can't stay,' she whispered angrily. 'Don't you understand? Please try to get up. We must go.'

'Lizzy.' May was crying.

Lizzy stared wild-eyed at the flames, and the flickering light it cast on the ceiling.

'Those stupid jewels. You're just like Mr Gains, wanting them. Leave them; they're not worth it. May and Charlie are in danger. We have to go to the village. We'll be safe there.' Despite her promise to help the boy, her brother and sister were more important. 'Abel, please, this is your last chance, then you're on your own. I'm sorry.'

'I am going home,' Abel said firmly. He was adamant and exhausted. He closed his eyes, and a calmness came across his battered face. He looked at Lizzy, then Charlie, and lastly at May and said, 'You must leave. Go before it is too late. It is me he wants. I will be all right.'

'Come with us,' May said, crying as she pulled his arm.

'Yes, come,' Charlie took his other arm. 'We'll help you.'

'I cannot, but you must go. Thank you for everything you have done. I shall be forever grateful. I just need to get to the east wing. It is not far. I'll rest, then I will get there, and I will be safe.'

'They'll look after you in Holcombe House. We'll make sure that. Nobody will hurt you there. And I promise we'll visit every day. We will, won't we Charlie, won't we May?' Lizzy said in tears.

'Yes, we will.'

'Yes, we promise.'

'I cannot,' Abel whispered.

'Please come,' May whispered as she cried.

Abel touched the prancing hare. 'It is beautiful, Munch.'

He was staying. Lizzy understood that now. The realisation was like a blow from a fist. She couldn't make him leave and had no strength to fight him, nor could they remain with him. The fire lit up the rooms, and soon, the whole building would be ablaze, just like the ones they saw from Hampstead Heath when they watched the East End of London burn after the bombings.

Lizzy grabbed the little ones and walked away. Charlie and May protested, but she ignored them and pulled them along. Betraying the boy by abandoning him in his hour of need was awful. She had no choice. Looking after Charlie and May was paramount, and staying would be suicide.

'We can't leave him,' Charlie cried.

'We can't.' May struggled against her grip.

'We must.'

She looked back, hoping to see Abel following, but he leaned against the wall with his eyes closed.

# Chapter 44

When Edith Gains reached the village and found the doctor, the blaze from the manor was visible as a dull light against a black sky. Ted was summoned by telephone, and by the time she told them what happened, the ruin burned brightly. She told her story in fits and starts and was comforted by the doctor's wife. The doctor took the salient facts in a few seconds and went to the lodge ahead of them.

Before long, Ted and Edith Gains went back as well. They saw the German lads who worked on the asylum gates in the town square. They had slipped their guards to watch the blaze. The fire had taken hold and lit the sky with an orange glow. Ted shouted at them with the few words he knew in German and waved his hand, '*Komm* now, *komm.   Schnell.*   Come   on,   lads. *Schnell*,' and they followed him.

'Damn it. It looks like the old place has gone. The fire brigade will be no use when they get there. What's Billy done now, girl?' Ted cursed Billy and his infirmities as he struggled up the hill.

'Oh, Ted. What ain't he done. He's gone stark raving

mad is what he's done. He'll kill that loony boy, the mood he's in.'

'If he kills anyone, he'll pay for it with a rope around his neck. What about those pups? Where are they? He ain't done nowt to them, has he?'

'I think they went to the manor with the boy.'

'Foolish kids. Why didn't you tell me that before?' He saw the blaze was consuming one end of the house, the flames crawled high into the night sky.

'There's more to tell you yet, Ted,'

'It'll keep, girl. Let's get to Miss Inglestone first. Here you two. Go to the manor. See what you can do. You understand?' He pointed, stabbing his fingers towards the flames. 'The manor. Two girls and two boys are in there, *zwei* girls and *zwei* boys. Damn it, lads, they're in the manor. Go find them. *Finde sie.*'

The soldiers followed his pointing finger.

*'Ja, Ja. Zwei Mädchen und zwei Jungen—wir finden sie—we find. We find,'* one of them shouted, and they ran towards the burning building.

# Chapter 45

Lizzy reached the ground floor, and the smoke was a choking fog, forcing them to move into the grand ballroom to escape. They held hands, with Lizzy in the lead. Their eyes stung, so they held handkerchiefs over their faces. Flames licked across the floor, forcing them further away from the main door while the great staircase was ablaze behind them.

'I'm scared, Lizzy,' Charlie cried.

'We're almost there. Once we get into the ballroom, we can get out through the windows.'

'What about Abel?' May cried.

'We couldn't stay with him.'

'But it's Abel.'

'Stop it, May. Come on, we're almost out.'

They entered the ballroom coughing and spluttering. The air was grey with smoke. Lizzy stopped when she saw Mr Gains and Sabre. The dog growled, and Bill Gains spun around. His dark eyes narrowed, and he slipped Sabre's chain. The dog flew forward, made mad by the fire, and bounded across the floor towards them. They screamed and pressed closer against the wall as

Sabre sensed their fear, snarling and gnashing his teeth. He crouched, ready to spring. Lizzy stood between the dog and Charlie and May.

'Seek, Sabre,' Bill Gains shouted in a drunken slur. He was almost crying. His pent-up anger and his years of being denied surfaced in a vicious shriek. 'You toffee-nosed bitch. It were fine before you came.'

'Get your dog off.' Lizzy's petrified eyes followed the confused and frightened animal.

'I would have had him and the jewels if it weren't for you. Where is he? Tell me if you know what's good for you.' He shouted, spitting out the words and stumbled in a drunken rage, landing on his hands and cursing again.

'I don't know. Please, Mr Gains, get Sabre away from us.'

'They're mine, do you hear? I'm the one who sweated for them all these years.'

As if emphasising his master's remarks, the dog growled at them but didn't know what to do.

'Leave us alone. We don't know where he is.' Lizzy shouted.

'Still trying to make a fool of me?'

'He's in the mansion, but we don't know where. Now,

please, get your dog away.'

Bill Gains grabbed Lizzy's wrist and twisted her arm until she screamed.

'I'll break it. Tell me, where is he? I've done for her. That old lady. I killed her. Do you hear? So, what've I got to lose, missy. Nothing.'

'I don't know where he is,' Lizzy screamed in pain.

'Leave her alone,' May rushed forward with Charlie trying to break his hold on their sister. Their fists flew as they attacked him, ignoring the barking dog, but their pathetic blows didn't trouble the enraged drunk.

He pushed Lizzy away and swung his fist in frustration. It went wild, careless and brutal, with no concern for where it landed. Catching May in the face, the force lifted the little girl off her feet and propelled her against the wall. She bounced against it and fell in a heap on the floor. Lizzy screamed in horror. Charlie dashed to his sister. Bill Gains stood frozen in disbelief, his mouth gaping. May was still.

'May!' Lizzy shouted.

She flew at Gains. Her fists pounded him, hitting him in the face, crashing against him, blow on blow. She screamed and spat, calling him any name she could think of and acting on instinct. She wanted to kill Bill Gains, to make him pay for hurting May.

Mr Gains just stood there. Ignoring the blows, he stared at the still body of the girl on the floor. Stepping back from Lizzy's rage, he was spent. His face was damp with sweat, and his hands were inactive at his side, the shotgun clattered to the floor.

Lizzy fell down beside May. She sobbed, crying for her to wake up and not be dead. Beside her, Charlie wept uncontrollably.

Sabre was barking at the ceiling, and Bill Gains withdrew from them. His face showed the fear of what he'd done, but when he looked up, he saw Abel. The boy was looking down at them, his face contorted with rage. He shouted at Gains, but above the crashing noise of the fire, nobody heard except Sabre.

Bill Gains came out of his stupor and was off, running as fast as he could to the burning staircase. He was going to find Abel. Nothing else mattered, not even the diamonds. The frightened and dangerous dog leapt after him.

Lizzy shook May, begging her to wake up. She didn't hear the crackling flames anymore or Charlie crying. All she could focus on was her sister's limp, broken figure. Time seemed to have stopped while the manor burned. It was her job to look after May, and she'd failed.

# Chapter 46

That was how Dieter and Karl found them. Lizzy was kneeling over her little sister while Charlie sobbed beside her in the smoked filled ballroom.

'*Mein Gott. Was ist passiert?*' Dieter pulled Lizzy to one side while Karl gathered her up next to Charlie. He placed his ear to May's heart listening, and then he opened her eyelids. He felt for her pulse and held his thumb up to the other boy, '*Sie lebt, sie lebt.*'

'What is it?' Lizzy shouted, pulling his arm.

'*Sie lebt,*' he said with a smile to reassure her. 'Alive. Doctor. Come. We must find doctor. The fire, *schnell*. Quickly. We go.'

Lizzy felt lightheaded and struggled to breathe. 'This is my fault. You and May should never have come with me, Charlie. May, I'm so sorry.'

Karl lifted May, cradling her head against his chest, and took her to the window.

'What about Abel?' Charlie grabbed Karl's arm, 'Abel is still here. Our friend is here somewhere. Mr Gains will kill him if he finds him.'

It took Karl a few seconds to understand his words.

'*Dieter, wird den Jungen finden*' said Karl. 'He will find boy, we go.'

'Is she all right?' Lizzy cried.

'Find doctor. Quick. Come.'

They climbed through the window, and Lizzy was the last to get out.

Karl carried May across the snow to the lodge. Their way was lit by the flames. He followed the Allens' chartered path, and Lizzy fell behind as they arrived at the lodge. The fight left her, and she struggled to keep up. Her legs dragged the dead weight of her body. Her arms hung limp, and her mind was a blank. She and Charlie wept tears that froze on their faces in the icy wind.

'Upstairs, to the bedroom,' the Doctor said as Karl carried May inside. His training made him calm, and he didn't react emotionally to the sight of the broken child. Edith Gains slumped in a chair when she saw May, and knew it was her husband's doing.

The doctor fussed over May, and Lizzy and Charlie, smoke-blackened and worn out from terror and anguish, huddled together as they watched.

'This is my fault,' Lizzy whispered. She prayed and made every promise she could think of, so that May would recover.

Ted put a hand against their backs to steer them away, but Lizzy hesitated.

'There's nowt you can do, lass. Let the doctor do his work.'

They went to the kitchen and sat at the table. The sight of Mrs Gains didn't trouble Lizzy anymore. But Edith Gains couldn't look at anyone.

'Well done, lad,' Ted said to Karl. 'Were a good job you did,' and he shook the boy's hand.

Karl nodded with an embarrassed smile. He looked towards the manor and told Ted he would go and find his friend.

'Is Miss Inglestone okay,' Lizzy asked.

'She's still alive, lass. But how long she lasts is anybody's guess. Now, don't you be thinking about that. She wouldn't want you worrying about her. It was never her way. Now my little pups, let's get you some tea—my old mum used to say strong sweet tea's best for shock, and she knew a thing or two, she did,' the policeman said.

Lizzy was stunned and stared into space.

It was an hour before the doctor came down. He was frowning. His sleeves were rolled up as he washed his hands in the sink.

'I've done what I can. There's no more I can do tonight. She's been knocked about like a rag doll. All we can do is wait and see. I'm sorry, young lady, but that's the best I can say. She's asleep now. I've given her something to keep her down and something for the pain.'

'Is she going to die?' Lizzy asked, fearful of the answer.

'Nay lass,' said Ted, and he looked at the doctor for reassurance.

The doctor sighed. 'She took a mighty blow. I can't do more. I'm sorry to have to say that, but the truth's best at these times.'

Lizzy and Charlie burst into tears, and Ted held them as they buried their heads into his chest, with their bodies heaving as they sobbed.

'There's never a good way of saying these things, Ted. You need to contact their parents. They should be here in case of the worst.'

'What about Miss Inglestone?' Ted asked.

'The nurse will stay to tend her and the lassie. I don't expect her to last the night. If she were younger, she'd have a good chance.' In a flat voice, he said, 'Ede, if the young lassie wakes in the morning, see she takes a little soup.'

Edith Gains nodded, but Ted shook his head.

'Sorry, Ede. You're coming with me tonight. I'll have to lock you up until we can sort things out. Milly's coming over. She'll look after these pups until I get word to their parents.'

'This is a bad business, Ted. It's bad business, for sure. Send for me if anything happens. I won't be sleeping tonight.' The doctor put his coat on to leave.

'The boy is still loose?' Ted said.

The doctor nodded. 'I'll go to Holcombe House tomorrow and check if he's turned up.'

'And if he's not, I'll search the manor—or anything left of it. It'll save us a lot of trouble if that Bill Gains has perished. Sorry Ede, but it's true, and there's no denying.'

When they went outside, the fire had taken a greater hold. As they watched, the manor shook and groaned in collapse. The booming noise of the crash reverberated against the walls of the lodge. Vast flames flared up through the shattered roof, and billowing smoke rose in a pall into the orange sky.

They saw Dieter and Karl coming back through the choking smog. Their faces and clothes were blackened, and their heads were bowed. The doctor sighed and removed his jacket.

'A bad business,' he muttered as Ted and Edith Gains walked away.

# Chapter 47

The day dawned sombrely, and the manor stood like a blackened shell smouldering against an iron-grey sky. The stench of smoke clung to the air.

When Milly arrived, she made Lizzy and Charlie breakfast, but it congealed uneaten on the plate. She did her best to cheer them up, saying her cooking wasn't that bad, was it? But her efforts were in vain. She understood they wanted to be left alone.

Lizzy scolded herself. She was overwhelmed by the guilt. Her mind was confused but tortured her remembering everything that led to her sister lying on the verge of death. Her mother made it clear that she was the eldest and, therefore, in charge. What a mess she'd made of that. She should have insisted Charlie and May stay behind. It was her job to look after them and no one else's.

Charlie followed Lizzy everywhere she went, staying close to his sister, and he was afraid to be anywhere else. He was lost.

Lizzy couldn't keep still and stood in the doorway watching May. The tiny girl looked so frail, with her head bandaged, nose taped, and the facial bruising. Blue-black welts appeared in blotches around her eye. Her breathing was soft, hardly raising the blankets covering her. And sometimes, she lay so perfectly still that Lizzy thought she had died. The panic was only quelled when she saw the gentle rise of the blanket again.

'Is May going to die?' Charlie asked softly.

Lizzy didn't answer; her hopes were ebbing away.

The doctor came to check on both patients later. He came downstairs with the same dour look. May had not woken up, and he spoke to Milly before seeing Miss Inglestone.

Lizzy followed the doctor and was crushed as he fussed around the old woman. Like May, she was still and silent. Lizzy looked at the friendly faces peering down from their lofty framed perches on the walls. A gentle reminder of happier times. Miss Inglestone was surrounded by memories, and Lizzy hoped they could somehow bless her with the strength to wake up. How scary the old woman seemed that first day. It seemed like such a long time ago.

She noticed the look on the doctor's face. It was one of despair. He whispered to the nurse and then shook his head when he saw Lizzy.

'I'm sorry, young lady. I don't think she'll wake.'

Numbness invaded Lizzy's mind. It left her silent and hopeless. She saw the world as if through someone else's eyes. She was detached as she watched the doctor bandaging Dieter's burned arms. She saw him in conversation with Ted and the slow shaking of his head. Even Ted had grown older since yesterday.

'I've sent a telegram to your mother,' Ted said to Lizzy. 'She'll come as soon as she can. It's difficult because of the lack of trains running over Christmas. With all the drama, I'd forgotten what day it was. It's Christmas Eve, ain't it, Milly?'

'Aye,' Milly said sadly.

'Not one to celebrate, is it, lassie?'

They waited. What else was there to do?

Dieter and Karl stayed throughout. They leaned against the kitchen walls, did whatever chores were asked of them, and waited. Every now and then, they went outside for a smoke. They wanted to be there, and Ted spoke to the camp commander to allow them to remain.

Lizzy thanked them for rescuing May. She apologised for not saying it earlier and admitted that she'd forgotten.

Karl gave a slight bow and smiled. She shook his hand and Dieter's and then sat down to wait again.

When the doctor returned, his tone was grave.

'I went to Holcombe House. The young lad is still missing.'

Ted nodded, understanding him. 'There's no hurry to search, I suspect.'

'And Billy? Any idea about him?'

'A Major Baines is coming over from army HQ to speak to the German boys. He speaks fluent German. We'll find out what the lads saw.'

The doctor sat next to Lizzy and Charlie and said, 'You have to be brave, lass. We can only wait and see— and that's the hard part. The nurse will stay with your sister, and I'll keep coming back.' He looked to Ted for help, but the policeman dropped his head with a gentle sigh.

'Can we see her?' Lizzy asked between her tears, and when the doctor said yes, she tried to get up. Her legs wobbled, and she almost fell over. She had to hold the edge of the table to steady herself. Ted reached out and supported her. Then, clutching Charlie, Lizzy followed Milly upstairs.

May's condition hadn't changed. Her bandages were fresh, and that was the only difference. Lizzy and Charlie sat beside her and held her hands.

'Please don't die.' Lizzy whispered.

She looked at Charlie but only saw the emptiness in her brother's face.

'It's not your fault, Lizzy. It's Billy's. You remember that. There's nowt you did were wrong. It were all his fault and no one else's.' Milly said.

If Lizzy heard her, she didn't react. She couldn't shake the blame from her mind.

# Chapter 48

Dorothy Inglestone died the next day.

It was Christmas Day. She'd defied the doctor and woke asking for Lizzy. She was weak, and her mind wandered, but her eyes were as sharp as Lizzy remembered that first day.

'Elizabeth. Abel is safe. He's told me. I thank you, Charlie, and May for helping him, as he thanks you. He told me he would be forever grateful for your help. He is so happy to have met you.'

Her eyes wandered around the room and rested on a photograph of her father. She reached out her hand, and Lizzy passed the picture to her and held her hand tenderly. Her face was dark and her vision distant.

'Daddy, I know. I was so glad.'

'She's rambling again, miss. She's been doing it on and off all night. I don't think she knows where she is. Or even when,' the nurse said.

'I've kept my promise to look after the children, Daddy. I did my best.' She saw Lizzy looking at the photograph on the bedside table. 'Elizabeth—is he not handsome? We lived in a beautiful white villa. You see, I was young once too.' Her body stiffened, and she grasped Lizzy's hand. 'It is gone Elizabeth—the door. It is gone forever.'

'Miss Inglestone?' Lizzy looked at her, puzzled.

The old lady lay back with a contented smile on her face.

Lizzy ran out of the room in tears. She'd suffocate if she didn't breathe fresh air again. She had to leave the house of sorrow and be outside. Standing on Miss Inglestone's patio, she looked to the wreck of the manor. She blinked like an owl in daylight, clearing her eyes of tears.

The next moment Charlie rushed out in a rage.

'It's your fault. Yours and Mum's. I didn't want to come here. Neither did Munch. You said it'd be okay. We should have stayed at home with the bombs. Miss Inglestone is dead. She's dead, she's dead. And Munch will be next. It's all your fault and Mummy's.'

Charlie ran inside the house before Lizzy could say anything to comfort him.

She was crying again, with huge sobs that she thought would never stop. The blood drained from her face, and her limbs were cumbersome. She dragged her sleeve across her face. When she looked up, Ted was standing beside her.

'Don't hold it against your brother. It ain't yours or your mum's fault. He can't help himself. He's young, and he don't know what he's saying. Miss Inglestone was old. She lived a good life. You need to remember that. She was a rare one, lass. You should have seen her when she were young—such a beauty. Aye, lass, Milly's right. I were in love with her. But then, so were we all.'

Before long, the undertakers arrived. A hearse drew up, and soon, two men aided by the German lads, carried a coffin out. They drove away, taking Miss Inglestone with them. Lizzy watched in silence. Milly crossed herself and muttered a prayer.

# Chapter 49

On that Christmas Day, the police searched the manor. It was a blackened hulk of shattered walls and smouldering pyres. The floors had collapsed into the cellars. They picked through the wreckage carefully, searching for Billy Gains and Abel.

Ted stood beside the blackened skeletal remains of a man wearing a ring on his little finger. The ring was gold with a soot-covered diamond that sparkled red when he polished it. Next to him was the skeleton of a large dog. Ted wore a sad expression for the rest of the day.

'Poor Billy.'

By mid-afternoon, as the light faded, they had searched the whole manor. Despite their efforts, they didn't find any other remains.

Edith Gains was back in the lodge. Ted didn't want to hold her in the cells over Christmas. She sat in stunned silence when Ted told her about their grizzly find. She didn't flinch or cry and was peaceful as if she already knew. It was not unexpected and the best outcome for Billy, she said. She told Ted everything that Billy had confessed to—killing Old Mr Inglestone in 1919 and starting the fire to hide his crime. He'd lied about seeing someone else there to avoid suspicion falling on him. She confessed that he'd stolen the ring and told Edith he'd found it. She couldn't bear thinking about May Allen and Dorothy Inglestone, blotting them from her fragile mind.

'Well, he's paid for it now, hasn't he? He always had a temper. I said it'd do him harm one day,' she said.

'It's unlikely you'll be charged with anything, Ede. I'm not sure you did anything illegal. They don't put people in prison for being mean and nasty. But you came right and tried to help Miss Inglestone. And you did your best to help the boy and the Allens as well. The Magistrate will decide in the end. It's out of my hands, but I'll put in a good word for you.' Ted said.

She nodded without any emotion. Ted made sure she didn't take anything that didn't belong to her as she packed her belongings and she left to stay with her sister in a nearby village.

Early the next day, Major Baines arrived. He spoke to the German lads for an hour. When he finished, he shook their hands, and they saluted him.

He found Ted, and they went into the kitchen. Lizzy sat with them. Her face was grey, her eyes red and swollen, and her clothes were a crumpled mess. She was silent and uncommunicative. Ted had said she should be there. It was the least he could do, knowing how much she cared for Abel.

'The one called Dieter has an active imagination. Put plainly, he says he saw the boy disappear.' Major Baines began.

'Disappear?' Ted asked.

'He saw Mr Gains having a go at the boy. His dog had hold of the lad's arm, and there was blood everywhere. The boy received a good mauling. He'll be scarred for life if he survives. Dieter attacked Mr Gains to free the boy. While they were struggling, the boy broke free and ran along the corridor. Anyway, the strange part is, he says he saw the boy leap through a door that wasn't there and vanish.'

'Vanish?'

Major Baines hunched up.

'Make of that what you will. His words, not mine—*Verschwinden*—vanish. He swears it happened but can't explain it. There was a lot of smoke coming from the doorway, and the boy just jumped into the smoke. Anyway, he said, Mr Gains saw it, ran after the boy, and went through the door. His dog went with him. He heard a scream and a yelp, and when he looked, they were at the bottom of a thirty-five-foot drop onto brick rubble and were dead for sure. He couldn't get down to find out.'

'Aye, well, we found them there, all right.'

'But them only, Mr Gains and his dog, and no one else?'

Ted nodded and whispered, 'Only them.'

'The lad can't be sure, there was too much smoke, and he was anxious to get away from the fire, but he thought he saw the boy again. He said he caught a glimpse of him running across the open land at the back of the building. He was sure it was him, as sure as he could be, under the circumstance. The boy was heading towards the high ground, in the direction of the moors.'

'Aye, we found a trail of footprints in the snow leading up.' Ted nodded. 'But any prints higher up were covered when it snowed again.'

'Well, make what you can of it, but that's what the lad says he saw.' The major rose, and Ted shook his hand.

'It'll make for a strange report. We'll put the boy's description out. He's going to need a doctor if he tangled with Sabre. We'll search again today, just in case. But if he's alive and wandered onto the moors, we might never find him. Them moors can easily take a fit grown man, let alone an injured boy.' Ted said.

'You'll organise a search?'

'As best we can with what we have.'

The policeman looked at Lizzy, who listened in silence. If she'd heard what they said, she didn't move. Ted walked the Major to his jeep.

'It was curious,' the Major said as he settled himself. 'The German lad said he thought he saw a room, like a nursery, just for an instant. He said it was after the boy jumped—and then it was gone. It must have been the smoke playing tricks.'

Lizzy wandered out of the kitchen and went to sit beside May. Charlie stood beside her. His head was down, and he took hold of Lizzy's hand.

'I'm sorry, Lizzy, I didn't mean what I said.'

'It's okay, Charlie. But you're right. I am to blame. I should have told the policeman where Abel was when he asked. Then Mr Gains would have left us alone, and Munch would be all right.' Lizzy hugged her brother.

# Chapter 50

Later on Boxing Day, Mrs Allen came, accompanied by Susan and a small, dapper man. They made their way to the police station, and Ted took them to the lodge, explaining what had happened on the way.

The sight greeting Mrs Allen broke her heart. May was silent and pale, her eyes were shut tight and her head wrapped in bandages. Her breathing was imperceptive. Lizzy and Charlie sat beside her, pale and wan as their little sister. They hadn't washed, their hair wasn't combed, and they wore the same clothes from when they ran to the manor with Abel, smoke dirty and crumpled. They burst into tears when they saw their mother and ran to her. They cried two nights of pent up anguish, sobbing uncontrollably, as she held them.

Lizzy wailed, 'I'm to blame. I wish it was me there and not May.'

It was as much as Mrs Allen could do to quiet them. But when she did, she sat them on Lizzy's bed while she held May's hand. She held her tears back with great effort. Now wasn't the time to cry. She looked at Susan, who understood her agony and almost broke down. Susan took a deep breath and went to Lizzy and Charlie.

'Okay, ducks. First things first. You both look a state. Wot? They ain't got no bathrooms up here? Or have you forgotten what one looks like? Get some fresh clothes, and have a bath. Come on now, we're here to sit with your sister and I ain't having no smelly, unwashed kids around me.'

They didn't want to leave.

'Now,' Susan barked. 'This won't do a bit. And no more blubbing. Bathroom—soap—clothes. And run a comb through those mops. You,' she snapped at the man who came with them. 'Get some food for these kids. Go on. See what there is in the pantry. Make yourself useful. This ain't no August bank holiday.'

When they left, Mrs Allen and Susan sat with May and prayed.

Before long, Lizzy and Charlie were clean, dressed in fresh clothes, and their hair had been washed and combed. They looked presentable, according to Susan— though she wouldn't want to marry them. She marched them downstairs and made them eat, nattering to Milly as she stood over them. When she was satisfied that they had eaten enough, she told them to go outside and have a dose of fresh air. It gave her time to talk to Milly, who told her the rest of the story.

'Thanks, Milly. That copper is all right, but he wasn't saying much.'

'She's got a nose for things like that,' said the man.

'She won't forgive herself, Mrs Allen won't,' Susan said to Milly, 'If anything happens to Munch, she'll never forgive herself that she wasn't here. But what's she to do?' She was annoyed with herself for not being there too.

'Get the tea on,' she said to the man.

'They say disasters happen in pairs, don't they?' Milly looked at the man suspiciously. 'I'll make the tea before we have another one.'

The children came in with the colour returned to their faces and the tiredness gone from their bodies, but concerns were still there. Susan talked about being brave, fearful that if they started crying, they'd all be at it.

'And that won't do. Not one bit, you hear me?'

# Chapter 51

The fretful night went slowly, as did all the nights since the fire. Mrs Allen sat up while Lizzy and Charlie slept in fits. She wept and prayed, and Susan kept the same vigil next to her. But May slept on, quiet and unmoving.

As the hours rolled by, they sat together, afraid to leave her for even a minute. The rising hysteria lurked so near the surface that it could so easily overwhelm them. In the quiet of the night, they were trapped with their thoughts. Somewhere in the house, the clock chimed every quarter, and the hours dragged. And as the night wore on, they became tired and pale, the blood drained from their faces. When the fire died in the grate, the room went cold, but neither made any effort to re-light it.

They didn't see daylight creeping in through the curtains or the sounds of the house rising with the hushed chatter from downstairs. Lizzy and Charlie woke up, and Susan took them downstairs and came back with coal to light the fire. She brought a cup of tea for Mrs Allen.

When the doctor came, Mrs Allen sat in silence as he busied himself. She watched as he put his instruments back in his bag and said there was no change and that he'd be back in the afternoon. She thanked him and resumed her vigil.

In her tired mind, Mrs Allen was playing with May, running through the house, playing hide and seek, or walking across the Heath. She saw the girl laughing at the ducks as they threw bread for them and how they scampered to get it. And she listened to May telling one of her long, nonsense stories. She'd tell them with gusto and exaggerated gestures. Every memory brought a rising tide of desperation. She struggled with her anger for the man who did this. How frightened May must have been. She held May's hand in hers and wouldn't let go.

May never wanted to come here and cried when told she had to. The doubts about sending them away came over her. She remembered telling them it would be an adventure like they read about before bed. 'And you'll be the heroine, my beautiful May blossom—it's your story,' she had said.

When Susan came back, she didn't feel the hug the maid gave her. Milly brought food, and it remained untouched and cold.

'She must eat something.' Milly pleaded with Susan for help.

By the afternoon, the doctor returned. And he was worried about Mrs Allen and spoke to her gently.

'You need some rest. It's not helpful if you get ill as well.'

But all he got was a vacant stare. She was unyielding and determined.

She would take May to Kew Gardens. When they got back to London, that's what she'd do. Then she'll buy her a new coat, her old one was threadbare and falling apart, and she's almost grown out of it. Then there was Marie's boat. She'd take the children on the Thames by Kingston. They'd love that. Especially in spring, when the weather was warm and sunny.

'Mrs Allen, you have to take care of yourself,' the Doctor said.

She didn't reply.

'I'll get Milly to bring some soup. Susan, make sure she eats it.'

Susan nodded.

'Mummy. I've had an awful dream,' a small voice whispered. 'There was a bad man, and he had a big dog. He searched for a diamond made from carrots, but not carrots you can eat. And a boy found it and hid it somewhere in a big house, and Lizzy was so brave.' May's eyes scanned the room and realised she was not in her bedroom at 32 Saltdene Road.

Mrs Allen burst into tears. Her head dropped onto May's chest, and she wept as the doctor fussed around the child. Susan held Mrs Allen, unable to speak.

'Tough as nails, that one,' the doctor said, a broad smile on his face, as he went into the kitchen. 'By all rights, she should be—well, you know. She's a fighter, all right. She's sporting a black eye that'd make any boy envious. Aye. Go and see her. She's awake and chatting like a good 'un. But not long, mind. She needs to sleep, and tomorrow I won't be surprised if she wants to get up and do something. You, make sure she don't,' he pointed at Lizzy and winked,

When she saw Ted and Milly laughing, Lizzy dashed upstairs with Charlie just behind her. Karl looked at the doctor.

'Aye—go as well, go on with you, the more, the merrier. You as well, young man,' he said to Dieter, 'No use being a wallflower, and you're all a part of it.'

Millie started crying.

'Ah, Women. Laughing and crying at the same time.

Go on, go and see the pup, you as well.'

The room was crowded, and May, the centre of attention, beamed at everyone, especially Susan. Milly found the prancing hare on a cardigan, and May clutched it in her fist, determined to never let it go.

'And when you're better,' Milly said, 'I'll make you some of those biscuits you like.'

'Here,' Susan, wiped away her tears, leant in and looked as sternly as she could at May. 'You ain't favouring someone else's biscuits over mine, are you, Munch?'

May grinned a missing toothed grin back at her.

'Well, I'll be. You're a traitor Katherine May Allen. And traitor's get their behinds smacked when they get home.'

'I'm glad to see you're doing well, miss,' said the man who came with Susan. He smiled at her.

May looked at him curiously, but smiled back just as broadly.

Mrs Allen left the room, and standing alone in the corridor, she wept again.

# Chapter 52

The next day, Miss Inglestone's funeral was held under grey skies. It was a simple service, and she was laid to rest in the family vault. No one said much, and Lizzy and Charlie were too sad to go inside. People that knew Miss Inglestone said she'd lived a full life, had travelled, had loved and been loved, and was never one to complain about life's vagaries. Though much of her life was spent in the Argentine, it was the village of Inglestone, named after her family, where she wanted to rest.

The mournful party returned to the lodge and moped around the kitchen as the doctor arrived and went to see May. The two German lads helped and got curious looks from Susan.

'Here,' Susan said to Lizzy, unable to quiet her curiosity, 'Who are these Jerries and what do they want—shouldn't they be in a camp or something? There's a war on, you know.'

When Lizzy told her about their involvement and how Karl had carried May back after rescuing them from the flames, she said, 'Well, knock me down, who'd have believed it?'

'They're good lads, and we had a good chat about Bonn, their hometown in Germany. It's where that geezer, Beethoven, was from. You know him, Susie, wrote that Da, da, da, dah tune,' said the man.

'Oh, had a good chat, did we? Since when do we speak German?' Susan rolled her eyes.

Seeing Lizzy's face, she nudged the man in his stomach.

'You ain't never met him before, have you? Strange, ain't he? Meet Mr Drake, me other half, and the bloomin' saviour of the human race. He's my old man. Now you know why we're winning the war, 'cause they ain't got him in the army, that's why.'

Mr Drake raised two fingers to his brow in a scout's salute and nodded to Lizzy.

'Nice to meet you after all this time, Miss Allen. I feel as if I know you. Susie talks about you all the time, she does.'

'You must come and have tea with us when we're back in London,' Lizzy answered politely.

Susan harrumphed. 'That'll be the day. Anything west of Poplar might as well be Australia, as far as he's concerned. His coming here is a bleedin' miracle. Took our May to be on her little death bed to get him out of his cot.'

'Well, I couldn't let your mum and Susie come on their own, now could I?'

Lizzy, Susan, and Mr Drake went to sit with May.

'Well, Katie, how are you doing?' Mr Drake asked,

'I don't know. No one ever tells me anything,' May said with a pout, and the man laughed.

'Well, this is a right to do, ain't it, Katie? I mean, it's been a right adventure. And I've heard you've been a little trooper. Blimey, what a black eye. You remember to duck next time. I should take me own advice, especially when Susie's on the rampage. She's given me plenty of them in me time. Here, let me have one of them biscuits, love.' He winked, and May sniggered.

He reached over and took one.

'And the treasure? Did you find it? If you did, don't forget your old mate, Arthur. Share and share-alike. That's my motto,' he laughed as he nudged her.

'Share and share alike? Mates? Don't you listen to him, Munch. You just watch out for his sweet talk—that's all them Drakes are good for,' Susan said.

Lizzy wandered out. It had been a topsy-turvy week.

She could barely make sense of it. She sat quietly in the garden and gazed towards the wreck of Inglestone Manor, trying to recall everything that had happened. Her mother followed her out and sat beside her.

'I'm so proud of you, Lizzy.'

But Lizzy was not feeling proud. She could still see Bill Gains striking May and remembered her helplessness.

'Don't,' Mrs Allen knew what her daughter was thinking. 'Do not feel that you let May down. Or Charlie. No one could have done a better job, and there's no one I trust more than you to look after them. None of this is your fault. Charlie and May trust you, and rightly so. They know you would walk a mile for them. I have never been prouder of you as I am now.'

Lizzy tried to protest, but Mrs Allen was having none of it. When she asked about Abel, Lizzy told her what had happened.

'Sadly, the policeman said that a boy is still missing from the asylum? They think he might be loose on the moors. They've searched, and they'll search again. The army is lending them a plane. But they fear he might never be found. I hear he was injured, and there've been some bitterly cold nights since. I'm sorry, Lizzy, I know how much he meant to you.'

'Miss Inglestone said he was safe.' Lizzy remembered how Miss Inglestone raved before she died.

'Safe?'

'It's difficult to explain, Mum. Miss Inglestone was convinced he'd be safe in the manor. In Abel's mind, the ruined manor was a better place than Holcombe House. But he must have left it when the fire took hold.'

'Do you believe he's safe?' Mrs Allen asked.

'Miss Inglestone believed it.'

'No, Lizzy. Do you believe it?'

'I don't know, Mum.'

'I have never met Miss Inglestone, but if what I heard about her is correct, I don't doubt her. So, you must believe it as well.'

'If only he hadn't gone back for the jewels, Mum, he would be safe.'

'I know, pet. But May will be her old self again, just you see. She'll remember it as a grand adventure, and so will you and Charlie, my darling.

The happiest sound Mrs Allen said she'd ever heard was when Lizzy broke down in tears of relief. She hugged her daughter and put her to bed to sleep a deep sleep, the first she had had for many nights.

Katherine May Allen slept happily and peacefully in the opposite bed, dreaming of a treasure they never found.

*Inglestone, North of England. One year later, December 1945*

## Chapter 53

'I never thought I'd see this bleedin' place again,' Susan complained. She peered out of the hotel window to the town, grey under a grey sky, and hurried back to the fire. 'Don't it ever get warm up 'ere, Milly?' As she poked the fire, a shower of sparks flew up the chimney. She stood with her back to it.

'I'll fetch some tea if you want,' Milly said.

'Nah, don't worry. I'll do it to stop me joints from stiffening. Where's those kids got to?'

'They went for a walk,' Mrs Allen said, just as the door flew open and Lizzy, Charlie, and May came in, wrapped in coats, scarves and gloves. Their faces were rosy with the cold.

'Sorry, we're late. We went up to the lodge to have a look and then walked around a bit. We lost track of time,' Lizzy said as she unwrapped herself.

'It's all gone, Milly,' Charlie said.

'The manor? Aye, they took it away during the

293

summer. Dug up the foundations and carted the lot off. The council's building houses there soon. And the lodge's boarded up waiting for new owners. Nowt to see anymore, I'm afraid.'

'Holcombe House is still there,' Lizzy said.

Milly huffed. 'More's the pity. They never did find the boy. They searched long after you left, but I hope he's happy now—wherever he is.'

'And we went to the library, but it was closed,' Charlie said,

'Oh, aye.' Milly smiled. She picked up a book next to her handbag, *A History of the Inglestone Family,* and Charlie's face brightened. 'Is this what you wanted, maybe? I thought you might. I reckon you can keep it. I can't see anyone else needing it.'

As she handed the book to Charlie, Lizzy said, 'Miss Inglestone said they'd be forgotten.'

'Not by you lot, I reckon,' Milly said.

A thin gentleman on the sofa cleared his throat too loudly. He was dressed in a black suit as if he'd just come from a funeral. He could pass for one of the mourners. His tie was black, and on his feet were shoes that had seen better days but were polished to a gleaming black sheen. Even his socks were black. He carried a black briefcase and held a black homburg. Unlike his attire, his face was pasty white and didn't look very healthy. He made up for that with a shock of black hair slicked across his head. He got up, a nervous and hesitative reaction, and arrived at an awkward posture—half standing and half sitting.

'Braithwaite. Jeremiah Braithwaite,' he announced to Lizzy. There was a moment of uncomfortable silence. He filled it with a nervous laugh and a cough. A weak smile broke his lips. 'From Brackenridge and Brackenridge Solicitors. Miss Allen, I presume.'

'And Mister Allen,' Charlie interrupted.

'And Miss Allen,' May said.

He gave a nervous laugh.

'So, Mr Braithwaite, from Brackenridge and Brackenridge Solicitors, here we are as per your request. It was an interesting letter you sent, bringing us all this way. Perhaps you can tell us what it's all about,' Mrs Allen said.

Jeremiah Braithwaite tapped his hat against his knees. 'Well, Mrs Allen, it's a bit strange.'

Mr Braithwaite fished in his briefcase and produced a

brown paper parcel, wrapped and folded, tied with strong twine and knotted. The package was old and had picked up stains over the years. It was twelve inches long, six inches wide, and four inches deep. In a carefully written copperplate, with the ink long faded, were the words…

For Elizabeth, Charles and May (Munch) Allen.

'We've got this parcel for, well, for your children.'

'I see. It is their names.'

'You don't understand. That's not the half of it.' There was a hint of excitement in the young man's voice. 'Aye, Mrs Allen, there's more. The firm that is Messrs Brackenridge and Brackenridge has been holding this package for a while. You'll see what I mean when you read this.'

He withdrew a piece of parchment paper, folded and firmly creased.

'It says here,' he said, reading the note for them. 'This parcel will be given to the Allen children on 24th December 1945. But stranger still is when it came into our possession: It was mailed to us on the 14th of May—way back in 1919.'

'What? 1919? Do you mean you've had this parcel for 26 years? And that it's addressed to my children? Mr

Braithwaite, they were not even born in 1919,' Mrs Allen said. It had taken her a second to understand what the man said.

Lizzy gave Charlie and May a puzzled look. Then they all looked at Mr Braithwaite.

'Yes, Mrs Allen, right odd, yes?' he said, nodding. 'But that's not all, there were more.'

'Is this a joke?' Lizzy asked.

'No, Miss Allen. We don't joke at Brackenridge and Brackenridge.'

'But since May 1919? That's impossible.'

'It's never been opened. You can see the knots still tied, and it's real firm. We stored it as requested. Aye, since 1919.'

There was a hint of satisfaction in his voice. He gave her the parcel—a job well done.

'Thank you,' Lizzy said, words deserting her.

'Is there something to sign?' Mrs Allen asked.

He placed a document before the children, who signed it and the copy.

In the silence, Mr Braithwaite realised he was no longer required. With a longing look, as if he wanted to see what was in it, he walked to the door that Susan held open for him.

'You got some strange ones up here, Milly. Bleedin' queer bloke gave me the creeps,' Susan said after he'd gone. 'Lizzy, you were born in '31?' Lizzy nodded. 'So what's going on?'

Everyone gathered around the parcel. Mrs Allen felt that since Lizzy was the eldest, she should be the one to open it.

Lizzy peeled back the brown wrapping paper to find a polished wooden box. It was locked, but a key had been provided. When she turned the lock and opened the box, Lizzy gasped, and almost at the same instant, both Charlie and May did the same.

Lizzy's hand trembled as she held the object in the box. It glinted in the electric light and cast a warm shadow on her palm. She passed it around in awe and amazement. It was a pendant with an enormous red diamond surrounded by smaller ones in a gold setting, and it shone in their hands.

'Blimey,' Susan mouthed.

On a note, and in the same handwriting as the parcel, were the words:

*For my friends, with gratitude and love.*
*From the master of Inglestone Manor.*

'What does it say?' Mrs Allen asked.

Lizzy lifted her gaze. She looked at Charlie and May. Then her eyes slid towards the window and stared to where Inglestone Manor once stood. Charlie's eyes followed hers. But May couldn't take hers off the jewels.

'It's the treasure,' May whispered.

## Author's notes

During the Second World War, and between September 1940 and May 1941, Britain was subjected to a sustained bombing campaign known as the 'Blitz'. Afterwards, there followed intermittent air raids, and from November 1943 to January 1944, another period of bombing called the 'Baby Blitz' came. If, at the end of this, the civilians of London thought their ordeal was over, they were mistaken.

From June 1944 until March 1945, London was subjected to attacks by flying bombs (V1) and rockets (V2).

Between 1939 and 1945, there were three significant evacuations of children to safer areas in preparation for the bombing of high-risk cities. The first was in September 1939, but by January 1940, almost 60% of those evacuated had returned to their homes. The second round of evacuations occurred in June 1940, and 100,000 children were evacuated (in many cases, re-evacuated). And when the Blitz began in September 1940, even more, were sent away. In June 1944, at the start of the V1 and later V2 attacks, an estimated 1 million women, children, elderly and disabled were evacuated from London.

This novel is set in late 1944, during that final wave of attacks.

# Acknowledgements

Many, many thanks to all of those whose contributions have helped me in writing *Inglestone Manor*. If I may pick out a few, I would like to thank Clare Newton for reading the first and unedited version that was grossly overlong—I re-read it when I was doing a round of edits and understood what a chore it must have been—so, her efforts were much appreciated, and to the team at Best Book Editors (Lynda Lyndhurst, Katherine Black and Sooz Simpson) who did such a fine editing job—any mistakes you might find are my very own, as I tinkered afterwards. And lastly to Clay Kelly, author of the *Beyond the Doors* children fantasy series, and Mitchel Maree, author of the *Magic Cube series,* for their helpful advice.

**Novels by S S Saywack**

The *Mary Finch Mystery novels* are a series of adventures written by S S Saywack.

Set in 1893, and in the mysterious world of Sherlock Holmes, they chart the adventures of Mary Finch, a fourteen-year-old maid, and her friend Archie Dibble. In dark and dangerous Victorian London, Mary must use her guile to survive.

*Mary Finch and the Thief*

*Mary Finch and the Grey Lady*

*Mary Finch and the Spy*

*Mary Finch Endgame*

*Mary Finch Runaway (a prologue)*

Available in both print and eBooks.

## About The Author

Originally from Guyana, a country in South America, S S Saywack came to London with his family in 1962. Educated in North London, he studied information graphics at a London college and then worked as a graphic designer for many years. He later changed careers and became a teacher at a sixth-form college in East London. Taking early retirement, he turned to a third career, being an author.

With a love for reading and history in general, he wrote his first novel that became the Mary Finch Series (four books for older children set in the fictional world of Sherlock Holmes) and that was swiftly followed by Inglestone Manor. His plans are to keep writing until he can't and to play the guitar (he does so, modestly) for just as long. His current writing scurries between children's fiction and adult detective fiction.

To find out more about S S Saywack, you can visit his website, https://saywackwrites.com/ or find him on Facebook https://www.facebook.com/SSSaywack/

www.blossomspringpublishing.com

Printed in Great Britain
by Amazon